Finding PERI GREY

MICHAEL GEORGE

STRATTON
—PRESS—
Publishing Life

FINDING PERI GREY
Copyright © 2020 **Michael George**

Stratton Press Publishing
831 N Tatnall Street Suite M #188,
Wilmington, DE 19801
www.stratton-press.com
1-888-323-7009

ISBN (Paperback): 978-1-64345-701-7
ISBN (Hardback): 978-1-64345-986-8
ISBN (Ebook): 978-1-64345-833-5

Printed in the United States of America

BOOKS BY MICHAEL GEORGE

Of Rain Barrels And Bridges
Horses Lemons And Pretty Girls

The Refuge Mystery series novels

Why A Refuge
Bridge To No Good
Grass Was Greener

CONTENTS

For Karren
I could never forget

For Mike and Carol
After a lifetime of friendship

For Jan and Paul
Very special people
With a very special family

CHAPTER 1

Even though it was much later than my normal five a.m. wake up time, I was still half asleep when the phone rang. Reading a good mystery had kept me awake late into the night, so I ignored the first couple of rings, hoping Mary would answer the damn thing. It took that long to remember once again that she was gone and had been for over a year, so I answered it.

"May I speak to Peri, please," said a polite voice on the other end after my hello.

"Who?" I answered, the name not registering in my foggy brain.

"Peri," she said, "Peri Gray."

The name registered this time. It should have, I'd known Peri since I was five years old, and that was a very long time ago.

"I'm sorry," I answered, "Peri isn't here. And the truth is, I have no idea why she would be."

"Well, she was supposed to be there. She said yesterday she would be at this number." The lady rattled off my phone number. "That is the number I called, isn't it?"

"It is, but there's still no Peri here."

"Is this the Dawson residence?"

"It is."

"Are you Ken Dawson?"

"I am."

"Well, she did give me the right number then. I've been trying to get her on her cell phone, but she's not answering. I have some very important information for her. If she does get there, tell her someone called with the information she wants."

"You can leave it with me. I'll give to Peri if she shows up."

"I'm sorry, sir," she said, her voice suddenly sounding tired. "I am not allowed to give out the information to anyone other than Peri. It would be highly unethical to do so. So be sure to tell her about this call if she does arrive."

The lady hung up, leaving me wondering what was going on. By the time I finished dressing, I knew my curiosity was going to make me crazy, so I called her brother, Bill, to see if he knew what the call was about. I didn't think he would mind since we were best friends all the years I knew Peri.

"Do you know what's going on with Peri?" I asked when he answered the phone. "Or why she is here in Tucson?"

"No on both questions. Why do you ask?"

"I got a phone call this morning from some woman who wanted to talk to her. The lady said Peri was supposed to be at my house. Peri wasn't, and I damn sure didn't know she was supposed to be. The lady on the phone said she had something important to tell Peri and wouldn't tell me what it was about, so I got curious."

"Well," Bill said, in his slow, meticulous way of speaking, "I guess I might be curious if I were you. I'm a little curious now too, because I don't have any answers to your questions."

"Do you have any idea what this might be about? Or what she might be doing in Tucson, if she in fact is in Tucson?"

"None whatsoever on any of it. I heard she was going to be gone for a while. I don't think anyone ever said why. We both know how Peri can be sometimes, so you know why I didn't ask."

"Yeah, I know. If you do find out, will you give me a call?"

"Of course, if I do find out. Other than that, how's everything down there in Arizona?"

"Pretty much the same, except that it has cooled down some now that it's September. How about you? Has everything frozen up there in Minnesota?"

"No, we haven't even had the first frost yet. I guess we are going to get lucky this year and maybe make through most of the month before we get one. We might even make it to October before we get a hard freeze."

"That would be for sure luck. Anyway, give me a call if you hear anything."

"Will do, and you do the same for me."

I always go for a walk first thing in the morning. Since it was already much later than usual, I decided to go. The house is close to Udall Park, which is large enough to make at least a two-mile walk without covering the same ground.

When Mary and I moved to Tucson, she retired and I only worked part of the time. There was plenty of work for a carpenter, but since I didn't have to work, I only accepted the work I was interested in, and then only if I liked the people who wanted to hire me.

That left me with some time to fill, so I needed a hobby. I took up photography. I started with a cheap point-and-shoot digital camera and found out it was a lot fun. I especially liked the way I could take all the photographs I wanted, and it only cost money if I printed them. But I quickly realized that a point-and-shoot just didn't do it, so I bought a couple of Canon DSLRs. I used one with a regular lens, the other with a telephoto lens. That way, I didn't have to change the lenses when I was out and about, hiking or whatever. It also became a habit to carry both cameras on the morning walk.

In Udall Park, it was possible to come across all sorts of animals. Anything from birds to snakes and lizards to rabbits, coyotes, javelina, or black bear. I'd only seen one black bear that wandered down from the Catalina Mountains, but I got a couple of good photos before he was caught and hauled away.

So as I always did, I took both cameras along. It was later than my usual walk time and there were a lot more people around than usual. That meant there were a lot fewer animals. I didn't see anything else interesting, so I didn't turn on either camera on this walk.

When I took the morning walk, I always left and came back in through the back gate. This morning, just as I was coming in, I heard a car door slam in the front driveway. I quickly walked around to the front to see who was there. The car was backing onto the street, and before I could get the driver's attention, it was heading down the road.

I went into the house through the front door and found a note taped to it. It was from Peri. I was extremely disappointed to have missed her even before I read it.

The note said that she was sorry that she missed me and that she would have waited around, but she had a plane to catch. I could understand why that would make her in a hurry, given the half-assed way the airlines operated, with their overbooking and all. Not to mention all the security bullshit one had to go through in airports. The note also said that she had planned on stopping over the previous night, but it had gotten late and she didn't want to bother me then. Peri should have known better. There was never a time in all the years we'd known each other when I wasn't glad to see her. The time of day never mattered. She ended the note, saying she hoped to catch me next time.

"What next time?" I wondered. This was the first time I knew about that she'd ever been to Tucson. At least not in the almost four years I'd lived there. So why would there be a next time here? Or she could have meant next time wherever, so I decided that was likely what she was referring to.

Inside the house, I called Bill. I told him about Peri and the note, and we again agreed we had no idea what was going on. We had little else to talk about, so we kept the conversation short.

I was hungry by then, so I made myself some breakfast and ate while I read the paper. After I loaded the dirty dishes into the dishwasher, I tried to figure out what to do with the rest of the day. Missing Peri was a real downer, so it was difficult to think of anything to do that could hold my interest.

I considered a hike up in the Rincon Mountains in Saguaro National Park, which was my favorite hiking spot. Hiking always made me feel better about life, but it was getting too late in the day for a decent one. Even though it usually cooled down some in Tucson in September, it was still going to reach the nineties before the afternoon was over.

I wandered through the house, in and out of the master bedroom, the guest room, the room that was Mary's office before she died, the living room, dining room, and kitchen. When I got to the craft room, which was originally a carport before I rebuilt and finished it, I decided to download the cards in my cameras onto my Mac.

It had been a while since I'd done it and it needed doing, so I hoped it would be a good time filler. I also wouldn't have to concentrate much while I worked.

After I finished the downloads, I went through all the pictures on the computer, deleting all the junk. There were always a lot of bad pictures. I was becoming reasonably decent amateur photographer, but I always took a lot of pictures. A large percentage of them were of wildlife on the move, so I was shooting fast. It meant that many of them were blurry and out of focus. I was always on the move too, so I never used a tripod. The anti-shake feature on the telephoto lens helped. I managed to take a lot of bad pictures anyway.

When I finished my first edit, I went through them again and printed out the few I wanted to use.

It was Mary who taught me the best way to use them. She retired when we moved to Tucson and needed a hobby, the same as I did. She was a brilliant seamstress, knew how to knit or crochet about anything, but as she said, "A person can only use so many clothes."

So she took up scrapbooking. She started working with old pictures, those of our life together and the pictures we had of her and me before we met. She also finished a couple of scrapbooks of ancestors, both hers and mine.

Initially, she worked on the dining room table. It quickly became obvious she needed a better workspace. That's when I remodeled the carport into the craft room.

Before she finished her first scrapbook, I realized scrapbooking would be a great way to use the pictures I was taking. With a lot of help from Mary, I took up the hobby too. After that, she continued to work with the old pictures and I worked with the pictures I was taking.

I hadn't done much of it since Mary died, so I filled the rest of the day catching up. It helped to keep my mind off Mary and how much I missed her, and once I got into it, I almost managed to push Peri Gray and the mystery she created out of my head.

Evening shadows were filling the house when I quit. I still didn't know what to do with myself, so I started going through my favorite scrapbook of all those Mary did. It was about the farm we owned in Minnesota. She did a fantastic job with it, from way she laid out the pictures, to the journaling and the background paper and matting she used. She covered it all. From the way the farm looked when we first bought it to the pictures she took just before we drove away in the rental truck with all our belongings to start our new life in Tucson, Arizona.

It brought back a lot of memories, mostly good, but also the reason we left it behind. Even though I missed the place, leaving it when we did was a good move. It gave Mary and me a lot more time together our last couple of years.

I didn't live in Tucson long before I realized I was real desert rat at heart. I could no longer even imagine living in Minnesota again, with its long, cold, miserable winters. As great a place to live as Minnesota is, I never wanted to spend another winter there. The hot, dry desert was my home now.

I grilled myself a large cheeseburger for supper and ate it with a thick slice of tomato, red onions, raw, and generous amounts of mayonnaise and mustard. I ate it on a hamburger bun, something I rarely did with Mary.

She was a type 1 diabetic, and the white flour and sugar in the typical bun or almost any kind of bread always raised her blood sugar to unacceptable levels, so we rarely kept any of it in the house. Because it was simpler, not to mention a lot healthier, I pretty much ate what she did. On those rare occasions when we were out and about and stopped for a burger or sandwich, she used the bun or bread as something to hold it with, peeling off the bread and throwing it away as she ate.

Most of the time, we ate a lot of vegetables, with a minimum of meat and fat, and small amounts of fruit at the end of the meal. She learned early that if she ate her fruit after the meat and vegetables, it didn't raise her blood sugar as high.

She was always careful to eat right and get plenty of exercise, so her blood sugar stayed as low as she could keep it. Lower blood sugar meant less insulin, and less insulin gave her a longer life. A longer life, anyway, than what most type 1 diabetics get. It still killed her in the end.

After I ate, I sat outside on my favorite rocking chair, drinking a cold beer and trying to finish reading the mystery that kept me up late the previous night.

Old memories and the little mystery Peri Gray created overshadowed whatever interest I had in how the book ended. When I finished my second beer, I gave it up, and feeling somewhat sorry for myself, I went to bed.

I was tired enough to sleep. It came hard anyway. Too many thoughts of Mary and Peri Gray jammed up my head. They were the only two women I ever loved. Mary was gone, and I was sure I would never really understand Peri.

My last thought just before I fell asleep was that maybe it was time I tried. What else did I have left to do in my life that could be more important?

CHAPTER 2

I woke up frequently during the night, and well before sunrise, I gave it up. I felt restless and unsettled, with absolutely no idea of what to do with myself. Everything that happened and everything I thought about the previous day hung over me like a dark cloud. So I decided to do what I usually did when I needed to sort things out. Hike the Rincons.

I filled my CamelBak with ice cubes and water and checked to make sure that there were enough snacks in the backpack with salt and carbs in case I needed them when I got up high. Enough water was the most important item, and I knew I would drink the near-gallon of water in the pack before the hike was over. I loaded the CamelBak, my cameras with backup batteries and extra memory cards, my wide-brimmed hat, and my walking stick in the car. I always carried a walking stick when I hiked. Having that third leg when the trail got rough was a definite asset. Especially going down a difficult trail.

I put on my hiking socks and boots, taking time to lace the boots up tightly, the way they felt the most comfortable to me. I didn't bother with breakfast. It was my usual habit to stop at Jack in the Box for a breakfast sandwich and some hash browns when I knew I was going to make the hike a long one.

I stopped for the sandwich on the corner of Pantano and Speedway and ate it on the way to the trailhead, which was on the east end of Speedway.

The first faint light of morning was peeking over the mountains when I drove into the parking lot. The empty lot told me it would be a decent hike. I always judged my hikes by how many people I ran across. The fewer, the better, and none was the best. Since it was a weekday, the chances were that I would be near the end of the hike before I saw anyone.

My favorite hike took a circular route, starting with the Douglas Springs Trail, picking up the Garwood Trail, then several others until I was back on the Douglas Springs trail, a lot higher. From there, it was a tough climb back down to the trailhead.

It was just over a six-mile hike, but as unsettled as I was feeling, I knew it wouldn't be enough. I took the Douglas Springs Trail the hard way, straight up into the mountains. I decided to hike to the campgrounds five point nine miles back, with an elevation gain of near three thousand feet, hoping the almost twelve-mile hike would clear my head some. The previous day's phone call about Peri, coupled with all the memories it dredged up, was haunting me a lot more than I thought it should.

As soon as I started, I could see the results of the reasonable amount of rain the monsoons gave us during July and August. The saguaro were standing fat and sassy on the desert floor, filled with the recent rains. The pads on the prickly pear were swollen and the cholla had lost the droop they so often carried during the extremely dry time of late May and June.

The ocotillos were leafed out too. It didn't matter what time of the year it was, if it was dry, they looked much like dead sticks poking out of the ground. When it was wet, they were covered with leaves. Now they were covering the desert floor and the mountainsides with a vivid green. The mesquite trees looked bright and sassy too.

Every place anything could grow contained some kind of plant life. Even on the steep, rocky cliffs, wherever there was a ledge or deep cracks, life found enough of a foothold to grow. It was hot, dry, hard country, but filled with more life than anyone who had never seen the Sonora Desert could imagine.

I loved it all, from the flat thorny desert floor, to the canyons, washes, cliffs, and steep rocky trails.

Because it was a quiet morning without any other hikers around yet, it didn't take long before I came across wildlife. There were about fourteen mule deer in the herd. Because I walk fairly quietly and I wasn't moving too fast, they didn't spook and run. Instead they pretty much ignored me, even when they heard the click of the cameras. Most of the time, when there were other hikers around, the best view of any deer I'd get was a look at their tails as they ran away from me at top speed.

I stayed with the deer for about forty-five minutes, constantly shooting pictures. I took about four hundred, and even got a couple of pictures of deer eating teddy bear cholla cactus. It was something I never saw before and wondered how they could do it. Teddy bear cholla are nasty plants. Their thorns are sharp and barbed on the end. I got too close to them once and got hooked. I had a devil of a time getting the barbs out of my hand and was bleeding a fair amount after I did. Those deer had to have incredibly hard mouths to be able to chew and swallow those things.

After I left the deer, I didn't see much wildlife. Only a few jackrabbits, running like hell, and some doves. The early morning desert air was still too cool for any snakes or lizards to be out.

I still took a lot more pictures, with the near perfect early morning light, and with a deep blue, cloudless sky for a background. I didn't seem to matter how may hikes I made in those mountains, there were always things I hadn't seen that had changed because of the rain or lack of it or that simply looked different because of the light.

It also never ceased to fascinate me the way the plant life constantly changed as I got higher. Somewhere around four thousand feet up, the saguaro disappeared and the scrub pine started to dominate the landscape. Up that high, there was a lot of open ground and I could see in any direction for miles. Most of the city of Tucson could easily be seen from there too, but it was the one view I didn't particularly admire. Tucson was spread over the desert in every direction. To most people, that was progress. To me, it was simply the destruction of the desert and all too many things that mattered.

I made fairly decent time for the rest of the way to the campground and only stopped to rest a bit at the high point of the hike. There the pines were a lot larger, yet nothing close to the size they were up another few thousand feet, where they grew tall and majestic. The air was cooler and the rainfall greater up that high, and it showed in the trees.

From the high point to the campgrounds, it was all downhill for at least a half mile. That part was nice. The trouble was, I had to climb back up, so I hesitated about going the rest of the way. It was my goal when I started though, so I went down.

The campground is very primitive and only sometimes has a water source. It all depends on the amount of recent rain and the time of the year. There's never a whole lot of rain in the Sonora Desert so I never found anyone camped there during the week, which was the only time I took this hike. The monsoons always came down fast and ran off just as fast, so there wasn't any water this time. The only time I ever found water there was when we got enough winter rain.

I took a long rest then, about fifteen minutes, and headed back. As it always did, the climb out of the canyon that held the campground was tiring, but once out, it was mostly downhill the rest of the way.

Even though I was beginning tire from the hike, it was a good, clean feeling that always comes with a long hike. It was a feeling I'd known countless times, one I actually appreciated, and had for many years.

I started walking and hiking fairly regular when I was in my teens. The habit started with Peri Gray. Our relationship was an off-and-on kind of thing during our early years. We were just kids in the neighborhood, sometimes playing together, either in groups or just the two of us. Nothing special or consistent, just kind of a childhood friendship, although I had a crush on her from the first time I met her, just a few days after my family moved into the neighborhood.

Then the teen years started. I was a year older than Peri and became interested in girls a bit before she was in boys. Even so, I was hoping I could convince her to be my girlfriend eventually.

When we had a minor accident together, things changed between us. School was recently over for the summer, and we were out on our bicycles, racing down a long hill with a sharp curve at the bottom. It was nothing new, all of the kids around the neighborhood did it on a regular basis. The difference this time was the patch of loose gravel we hit at the bottom.

I don't know which one of us lost it first, but suddenly, we were a tangle of bicycles and we both went down hard. I didn't feel any pain from my skinned-up hands, elbows, or knees right away. Peri stood up bleeding and all I felt was guilty and stupid, sure the whole thing was my fault.

"I'm sorry, Peri," I told her. "I didn't mean to do that. It's all my fault. I'm really sorry."

"I don't think it is," she said. "It just happened. Things happen. So stop saying you're sorry."

"But I shouldn't have…"

"Hey, I was having fun too. I guess we should go home now, though, and wash the dirt out of the cuts."

"I'm okay, but we should get you home. You're bleeding."

"Don't look now, Ken. So are you."

"I am?"

She laughed. "Yeah, you are."

We pushed the bicycles up the hill, with me constantly saying I was sorry the whole way. At the top, we found both bicycles in working order and rode home in silence. I felt terrible when I left her at her house and rode home sure that any chance I had of making her my girlfriend was lost.

Peri came over after supper that night. Her knees and elbows were bandaged, as were mine. Otherwise, she didn't look as if she had sustained any serious injuries from our accident. I was greatly relieved to see that, not to mention I was simply very happy to see her. Maybe she didn't hate me after all.

"Let's go for a walk," she said as soon as I was outside.

"Sure, where?"

"Over in the park."

What we called the park was just a big, nearly empty field about two blocks square. It was one of a very few places close to home that hadn't been developed yet, although it soon would be. There was a makeshift baseball diamond in one corner, a lot of open space, and a large patch of lilacs along the far side.

When we reached the park, Peri took my hand, squeezed it, then continued to hold it. It is impossible to describe all the feelings running through me. Peri Swenson (her married name is Gray) was actually holding my hand. *She must like me,* I thought. Maybe as much, I hoped, as I liked her.

We walked to the lilac bushes, and she led me inside, still holding my hand, until we stopped at a small clearing, completely surrounded by the bushes. She let go of my hand, and we sat down, facing each other.

Peri was never shy, and the first thing she said was "I want to be your girlfriend, Ken. I really like you. You're always so nice when stuff happens. You never blame anyone else for it. Do you want to be my boyfriend?"

"Well, yeah, sure, of course," I stammered. "I…I really like you too. A lot."

"Good." She smiled. "Then I'm your girlfriend and you're my boyfriend. But let's not tell anyone else. It's not their business, so we'll keep it a secret."

"Okay," I agreed. Anything she wanted now was okay with me, even though I knew it wouldn't be a secret for long. All we would have to do is spend a lot of time together and everyone in the neighborhood would know. That was something I didn't care about at all. Having her for my girlfriend was enough, even though I didn't have much of an idea what that meant, other than she liked me.

We stayed there for a while, then when we decided to leave, I kissed her on the cheek. She smiled, turned her face toward mine, and we kissed on the lips. It was a first for me, so it wasn't much of a kiss, but at the time, it seemed to be close to the most wonderful thing there was.

The kisses steadily improved as their frequency grew. It became our custom, when it was possible, to walk a lot farther than to the park. A little over a mile from home, we had a creek that flowed even during the dry of summer. The rapid development where we lived hadn't caught up with it, so it was still wooded on both sides. It was another mile walk upstream to a small meadow out of sight of the creek.

We spent countless hours there the rest of that summer, sometimes talking quietly, but most of the time necking, which for the first few weeks consisted of a lot of kissing and hugging. Until the day I impulsively reached over and put my hand on her breast as we lay side by side on our backs.

She gave me slight grin, and when she didn't object, I squeezed lightly. I was sure then, that I would never feel anything as soft and wonderful. She hadn't as yet grown into the woman she would soon be, so she wasn't wearing a bra. She didn't need one yet. I could feel a lot even with her cotton blouse covering her.

For the next few times we were there, I occasionally touched her, then finally got real brave and opened a couple of buttons and slid my hand inside her blouse. I thought I'd found perfection, until the day she let me take her blouse off and I could see her. That *was* perfection. I took off my shirt and pulled her close, knowing the wonder then of her warm skin touching mine.

That's as far as we ever went that summer, and all too soon, it was fall and we went back to school. Her family was Catholic. Peri, Bill, and their sister Judy and brother Steve went to the local Catholic school. I went to the public school, so during the week, we didn't see much of each other. As the weather turned from cool to cold, which happens quickly in Minnesota, it became almost impossible to find a place to be alone.

Saturday nights at the movies were about it, and they became less frequent as the school year wore on. Peri was involved in a lot of school activities, and I was busy working with my dad.

He was a carpenter and also had a small woodworking shop in the backyard. That winter, he often put me to work in the shop on weekends, slowly teaching me woodworking skills. I didn't mind doing it either because he paid me more than I could have made anywhere else.

When school was out in the spring, Dad started to take me along on some of his building projects, so my time with Peri was limited, although we occasionally did hike to the creek. It was never quite the same as it was the previous summer, and shortly before school started again, it was over between us.

"I'm not going there with you anymore, Ken," she told me. "I still like you and want to be your friend. That's all though, I met another boy I really like."

I was heartbroken but continued to hike to the creek alone when I got the chance. I kept the habit of walking and hiking as often as possible for the rest of my life.

Which was a real asset when it came to the last two miles of the Douglas Springs Trail. Just before I started the steep climb down, a Gila monster scooted out onto the trail just ahead of me. It was moving fairly fast, so I picked up the pace, hoping to get a few decent pictures of it. They are usually shy and are becoming rare, so I really wanted the pictures. I'd never seen one before.

Suddenly, the critter stopped and turned to face me, letting me know on no uncertain terms that it had had enough of me. I stopped too, knowing better than to get to close. They are poisonous, and when they bite, they do not let go. But I was close enough to get several pictures before it decided I wasn't worth bothering with and moved off into the brush on the side of the trail.

The rest of the trail down was filled with high steps, large rocks, and steep cliffs on the right side of the trail. Only the last half-mile was flat ground. By then, I was so tired that stretch felt like it went on forever.

When I got home, I put all my gear away and went out back with a cold beer. I sat down on my favorite rocker; the summer with Peri was still very much on my mind. That led to thoughts of Minnesota. I hadn't been there for a real visit since we moved to Tucson. Going up for Mary's memorial service didn't count. I was too far out of it when she died and didn't stay up there long enough for it to matter. It somehow seemed to matter now. It would be good for me, I knew, to spend some time with relatives and friends, especially Bill. Having the chance to spend an afternoon with him, talking about anything and everything over a few beers, was to me as pleasant a way to pass the time as there was.

And seeing Peri would be a real treat too, as would learning about her mysterious trip to Tucson.

CHAPTER 3

I wasn't sure what I was going to do when I went to bed, but when I woke up in the morning, there was no question. I was going to go to Minnesota.

I skipped my morning walk, something I rarely did. I ate a bowl of cold cereal for breakfast and then went outside to check out the RV.

The first thing I did was start it. I neglected it most of the time and hadn't had it running for couple of months. The battery was solid, as were the auxiliary batteries, so it fired up with no problem. I let it run to get a full charge in the batteries while I went inside to call the RV dealer where we bought it, to see when I could bring it in for a checkup. They had an opening in couple of hours, so while I waited, I flushed the water tank and refilled it.

The RV dealer had a good crew doing repair work, so my wait while they checked out all the belts and hoses under the hood, changed the oil, and gave it a lube job was only a little more than an hour.

Back home, I checked out the staples in the kitchen of the RV, started up the refrigerator, and filled it with what I could find in the house kitchen that I thought I might use.

By evening, I had a suitcase packed and loaded, my cameras and accessories, hiking gear, and everything and anything else I thought

I might need for the trip safely stowed away in the RV. Then I went over to my next-door neighbor to tell him I'd be gone for a while.

He promised to keep a close eye on the house and that I should have a good trip. He was a nice guy, not to mention a retired cop, so I never worried about the house while I was gone. It was just as unlikely that anything would go wrong with him watching it as it was when I was home.

I was getting real anxious to be on my way by then, so I drove the RV out onto the street and hooked up the small car that Mary and I bought just for towing behind the RV.

I didn't have to worry about blocking the road with them. The RV was only a twenty-two-foot Class C, so they both fit nicely in front of the house. The fact that they blocked my driveway was irrelevant.

I was in bed by eight, but just before I went, I called Bill to tell him I was coming. I thought about calling my son too and then decided not to. We didn't get along at all, and I figured if I called him, I'd have to listen to him bitch about something or the other for a lot longer than I wanted to spend on the phone.

I woke up about 2:00 a.m. and tried to go back to sleep for a while. It didn't take long to know it wasn't going to happen. I was too anxious about the trip. I was excited to get started, even if I was a bit nervous about making the eighteen-hundred-mile trip alone.

I wasn't all that confident in the RV either. Mary and I bought it shortly after we moved to Tucson. It was almost new, with less than ten thousand miles on it. We were hoping to do some serious traveling, but by then, Mary never felt well enough for more than a few short trips. It hadn't been used at all for over two years.

I tried to tell myself to stop worrying or think about it at all. Even if I did have a breakdown, I carried a cell phone for emergencies, and if by some chance I had a problem where there was no reception, I could always use the car to find help.

Almost convinced, I dressed, locked up the house tight, and left without bothering with breakfast. I knew I could get a sandwich at a truck stop when I got to Las Cruces, New Mexico.

Tucson was a quiet city when I started out. I didn't see another vehicle from the house to Pantano or on Speedway. I was on Houghton Road, almost to I10 before a car passed me, heading north. The freeway always carried some traffic, no matter the time of day or day of the week, but at that hour, it was sparse.

I took the RV up to sixty-five and set the cruise. At that speed, the Ford V10 purred along nicely, without immediately sucking the fuel tank dry the way it would at a higher speed.

I ran into a little more traffic going by Benson. It was mostly semis and all of them heading east flew by me. On the long climb coming out of Benson, I had to turn off the cruise control. It simply couldn't handle the constant gear changes on a road that steep.

I made my first stop at Texas Canyon. Not because there was any need, it was more because I always stopped there when I drove through, no matter where I was going. It was also interesting and held a quiet beauty, even with the large number of trucks parked coming and going or parked. I took a minute to look at the rock formations surrounding the rest stop. Then I used the restroom, something I always did when I made a stop while traveling, whether I needed to or not, and was on my way again.

The rest of the way to Las Cruces was uneventful. I cruised at a steady sixty-five and watched the traffic fly by me. I only passed one other RV, a large Class-A pulling a full-size sedan, that was having trouble on a short uphill climb.

By the time I reached the truck stop, I was somewhat sleepy, something that always happened to me when I was awake at sunrise. I filled the RV, bought a breakfast sandwich, and was on my way again. I picked up Highway 70 at Los Cruces, made another steep and long climb leaving the city, and followed 70 to Alamogordo.

From there, I took 54 to Santa Rosa, a two-lane highway with a speed limit of fifty-five most of the way. New Mexico has its own kind of beauty, and I always enjoyed driving this stretch.

At Alamogordo, Highway 54 became part of I40 for several miles. I filled up with gas at a truck stop right after I got on the freeway and bought a not-so-great sandwich there. Driving I40 was always far less than pleasant, crowded with trucks as it always is. They were mostly driven by people who seemed pissed off at the world. They were not about to give any quarter on that stretch of freeway. I stopped at the very crowded rest stop, as much to calm my nerves a bit as anything. I didn't need to, but I used the restroom and was on my way.

It improved a lot at Tucumcari where I left I40. Highway 54 was again two lanes, and the speed limit was lower. From there, I stayed with 54 through a small corner of northwest Texas and the Oklahoma panhandle.

I filled the rig in Liberal, Kansas, as much to stretch my legs and pick up another sandwich and a cup of coffee as to buy gas. I was getting tired, and I needed something to help me stay alert this late in the day.

Most people complain about how boring it is to cross Kansas. I always found it to be a nice drive. All the towns I drove through were well kept and clean, and the people were as friendly as anywhere else. But the long, straight stretches of road, the evening shadows, and the hours of driving caught up with me. Before I made it to Wichita and the Kansas Turnpike, I stopped at a small RV park. Driving any farther without some sleep was senseless. And I knew I'd make it to Minnesota the next day. I had less than eight hundred miles to go.

After I registered at the office and parked, I made myself a cheese and lunchmeat sandwich, took a quick shower, and crawled into bed, sure I would fall asleep right away.

Instead, I lay awake, reviewing the trip so far, and then spent even more time wondering how long I should stay in Minnesota. It would depend on how things went when I got there, I finally decided.

The one thing I knew for sure was that I would be back in Tucson long before there was even a chance of winter weather. It would be total misery to drive the RV, towing the car, during the winter. It was tiring enough now, with the good weather during this early September. I didn't even want to imagine driving through some of the bad weather I drove through so many times during the many years I lived in Minnesota.

I tried to forget the whole ludicrous idea. There was no way I'd ever let myself get caught doing something so foolish. Yet I did let myself get caught in bad weather under other circumstances, several times.

Working construction, I took on jobs all over the Twin Cities, and during the winter, it wasn't uncommon to end up driving home through some pretty rough weather. One of the worst storms I ever got caught in happened when I did a friend a favor. It was only a couple of months before I met Mary.

I was working on a framing crew in the northern suburbs at the time, not too far from where I lived. My friend was building a couple of houses in South Bloomington, a long drive through the city for me. His finish carpenter suddenly quit on him, and one of his houses was supposed to close in just a few days. He was desperate and wanted me to trim it out for him. I wasn't sure I could, so I called my boss to see if he could spare me while I did it.

Since the weather all through October and the first couple of days of November was beautiful, letting get us a bit ahead of schedule, the boss said I could have two days. After that, whether the house was done or not, he wanted me back on the job.

I was a good finish carpenter, even if I was nowhere near the fastest. Yet I was sure I'd get it done if I put in a couple of long days.

The first day went real well. The weather was great, still in the sixties with lots of sun, and by the time I quit that night, I was just over half done with the trimming. All the interior doors were installed, and the casing on the doors and windows was well on its way. I was sure that I'd finish with one more long day.

A light rain started on the way to work the second day, and by the time I unloaded my tools, it was snowing lightly. The temperature was in the low thirties. I didn't pay any attention to the weather after that. I pushed hard all day, and only took about ten minutes to eat the couple of sandwiches I brought along for lunch.

I made good time and completed the job about five that afternoon, just in time for rush hour. It was snowing hard when I loaded my tools into my pickup, but it didn't seem as though it would give me any serious trouble. I'd driven through worse weather.

I didn't have any problems until I got on I35. It was almost a parking lot going in both directions. As always happens during the first real snowfall every winter, most people had forgotten how to drive in it. They were stuck wherever there was a slight incline on the freeway, and the ditches were filled with the morons who weren't smart enough to slow down.

I knew I was going to get nowhere staying on the freeway, so I left it as soon as I reached the next exit, hoping to do better on the city streets. I didn't have any luck there either.

The snow steadily increased, and the wind was picking up. Even on the city streets, with all the lights, the visibility sucked. While I was trying to figure out what to do, I drove by an apartment building that looked familiar. I'd been there once with my friend Bill, and I remembered it because I wondered at the time why Peri would want to live in a building on a street as busy as Lyndale Avenue.

I wasn't even sure she still lived there, but given the circumstances, I decided what the hell, made a U-turn, and went back. If she was home, I was hoping she wouldn't mind if I killed a couple of hours in her apartment. By then, I was sure, the traffic and the snow would be light enough so I could finish the drive home.

She answered the door right after I knocked. She looked shocked when she first saw me but quickly smiled.

"Ken," she said, "what on earth are you doing here?"

"Snow," I told her, "lots and lots of snow. Not to mention a lot of people who damn well *do not* know how to drive in it."

"What are you doing here though?"

"I just finished trimming out house south of here and I got caught in the mess out there on the way home. Traffic is at a standstill right now, and as I was driving by, I remembered that this is where you live. So I stopped to see if it would be okay to wait it out here for a couple of hours. That is, if you don't have any plans or anything. If you'd rather I don't, it's okay."

"Of course, it's okay. I was going to go out with my boyfriend for dinner, but that's damn sure not important. Come on in. I'll call the boyfriend and tell him to forget it tonight. I don't really feel much like going out with him anyway."

I took off my coat and boots and sat on the couch while she made her call. She came back into the living room.

"Well," she said with a laugh, "that takes care of him for the night. The twit didn't want to go out in this weather anyway. His new car might get hurt."

"I just hope I'm not putting you out," I said. "I do appreciate you letting me sit here for a while. It's a lot more comfortable than sitting in the truck, stalled in traffic. I think it'll get a lot better in a couple of hours though."

"I wouldn't count on it, Ken. According to the weather on the six o'clock news, we're in for a lot of snow before it stops. They were talking about twenty inches or more."

"If that's the case, I might as well get moving now. There must be a motel around here somewhere."

"Don't be ridiculous. You *are* staying here. You can always sleep on the couch. It makes no sense for you to pay for a motel room. Besides, this the kind of a night when having some company will be fun."

"If you're sure it's okay?"

"Ken, enough of that already. You've always been so apologetic about everything. I like you for that, just don't overdo it."

"Okay. If I am going to stay here, then I think I'll run down to my truck and get the change of clothes I always carry along, just for times like this."

"I have a better idea. There's a bar on the corner that serves a good hamburger. Let's walk over there and have a burger and a beer for supper. I don't have much here to cook and don't feel like it anyway. You can pick up your clothes on the way back."

It was snowing and blowing even harder on the short walk to the bar, and I knew Peri was right. There was no way I was going to get home on a night like this.

The bar was nearly empty, so the waitress immediately brought us the pitcher of beer Peri ordered and wasn't far behind with our hamburgers and fries.

The beer was cold and the food was good. Watching Peri on the other side of the booth while we ate made it all even better.

"I guess," she said when we finished eating, "we should go. It's not getting any nicer out there, and I think they would like to close now."

"Okay," I agreed, finally noticing that we were the only people in the bar and that they were indeed, getting ready to close.

I picked up my change of clothes on the way back to Peri's apartment. The snow on the sidewalk was deep by then, and the only cars we saw were stalled or parked. There was no sign that the snowplows were running. The ruts in the snow left by the earlier traffic were barely visible, and the snow was rapidly building drifts everywhere.

It had been a long day already, so I asked Peri if it was okay to take a shower. "Well of course."

I showered and put on the sweats I carried with my change of clothes. Peri took her shower as soon as I was out of the bathroom. She joined me on the couch wearing a heavy flannel bathrobe over some kind of nightgown and carrying two glasses of dry red wine.

"Cheers," she said when she handed me mine. We clicked glasses and sipped the wine.

"It's sure nice of you, Peri, to let me stay here. I don't think I'd like it much out there on the highway right now."

She laughed. "More than likely, if you were, you'd be in a ditch somewhere."

We talked for a while, watching the heavy snow swirling around outside of her living room window in the now dim light coming from Lyndale Avenue. The talk was mostly about family and when we were kids in the old neighborhood. I skirted around the subject of our special summer, but Peri brought it up after a while.

"You know," she said, "I hate it the way it's been built up all along the creek. The place we used to go swimming, even that meadow where you and I spent so much time that one summer, are gone now."

I agreed about not liking all the development. Then I told her that she was the first girl I ever kissed, how I found it exciting just to hold her hand, and how I remembered that summer as one of the best times of my life.

"If you liked holding my hand and kissing me that much," she giggled, "then you must have loved some of the other things we did." She paused then, actually blushing slightly. "I know I did."

I felt my face warm some and was sure I was blushing slightly myself. I tried to find the right words to answer her, couldn't, and just grinned.

"I like it that those are good memories for you, Ken. I think it's really nice."

"They aren't just good, Peri. What they are is great, actually," I answered, still grinning.

"Well, good." She set her glass on the coffee table, took mine and set it down, then leaned over and kissed me. It lasted a long time. A very long time.

"I've always wondered," she said when we broke the kiss, "what we would have done if we'd been a couple of years older that summer."

"So have I. Maybe it's just as well we weren't. We could have ended up in some serious trouble."

"That's possible," she said, "but I still wonder."

She sat quietly on the edge of the couch for a while, just watching me. I watched back, having trouble meeting her eyes and having as much trouble keeping my eyes off her breasts. A lot of them were showing through her sheer nightgown, now that her robe opened a lot during the long kiss.

Abruptly, she stood, took my hand, and leaving the half-full wine glasses where they were, she led me to her bedroom. I just stood there, dumbfounded.

"No couch for you tonight, Ken," she said as she dropped her robe on the floor. "Now get out of those sweats."

I did as I was told, constantly staring at her breasts, her nipples showing clearly through her nightgown. She was definitely a lot more grown up than she was during our time in the meadow by the creek. My excitement from looking at her was obvious before I got into bed with her.

"My, my," she said as I pulled her close. "I think this is going to work every bit good as I've always been sure it would."

CHAPTER 4

I spent a restless night in the RV, waking up wondering what I was doing there. What gave me the impulse to go to Minnesota so suddenly? Did I really want to go there, or was the whole trip about finding Peri Gray? I'd known her almost all my life, why worry about finding her now.

Could it be because the time I thought I'd found her, I really hadn't? Not for any length of time anyway. Or maybe it was because that short time was as incredible as it was. The night I spent with her during the snowstorm was one I'd never forget. It didn't end there though.

I came close to jumping out of bed when I opened my eyes and noticed the dim light coming through the bedroom window. I was already late for work.

"What's up, Ken?" Peri sleepily asked as I sat up and swung my legs over the side of the bed.

"I think I'm late for work," I said. "It's daylight already and I've got a long way to drive."

She sat up, letting the covers fall away from her bare breasts, without a hint of shyness about it. As soon as she looked out the window, she laughed a little. "You might as well not worry about it. In case you haven't noticed, it's still snowing. Hard!"

"Yeah, you're right. I think I better call the boss and tell him I'm not going to make it today. There's no sense in pissing him off."

"I suppose you better. Just don't be too damn long on the phone."

My boss answered the phone right away, surprising me. I thought he would be out at the job site by then, no matter what the weather was. I explained my situation to him, but left out any mention of Peri.

"Don't worry about it," he said. "It's still coming down hard here and blowing like hell. Nothing's moving. I doubt we'll be able to do a damn thing before tomorrow morning, if then. Just get up here as soon as it's safe. We *will* need you. With two houses still open, we'll be at least a half day shoveling them out before we can pound even one nail."

"I'll get there as quick as I can," I told him.

Peri smiled when I got back into the bedroom. Neither one of us said a word as I got back in bed. I didn't think it would be possible to make love to her again, as often as I had during the night. Her power of persuasion was awesome though, so I managed quite nicely. I moved slow and easy, never wanting it to end.

Later, I made us breakfast out of the few eggs, some hotdogs, and bread in the refrigerator. It was anything but a gourmet meal yet tasted as good as any breakfast I'd ever eaten.

We sat down on the couch with our coffee to watch the snow fly by the window, pushed by a howling wind. I loved seeing that snow out there and found myself hoping it didn't end too soon.

The feeling of isolation, of Peri and me being in our own little world with nothing to do but sit close and soak up the pleasure of being together, was one of the greatest feelings I've ever had. The world and life with all its problems seemed far away and I found myself wishing it would stay there. After a while, she took my hand in hers and gave it a light squeeze, sending ripples of excitement through me.

"I think I'm still tired, Ken," she said. "Let's take a nap."

We did, not making love again until we both woke up. We spent the rest of the day like that, holding hands on the couch, short naps, and times of love.

The wind died down, and the snow slowed to flurries that evening. We went out to see if the bar on the corner was open and it was, so we ate burgers, fries, and drank a pitcher of beer again.

When we went back to her apartment, Peri asked, "Are you going to try to go home now?"

"Do you want me to?"

"No. If it was up to me, it would snow for another week."

"I feel the same way."

"Good. You can leave in the morning if you have to."

I had to. Peri had a sad, somewhat lost look on her face when I left. She took my hand as I went out the door, and trying to smile, she gave it a light squeeze.

I was the last one in the crew on the job that morning. No one said a word about my being late. The boss simply handed me a shovel and said, "Have fun. We all are." And it was fun, spending all morning shoveling snow out of the two open houses that had drifted in as much as four feet deep.

I was still thinking about the snow and that time with Peri when I left the RV park at barely three a.m. After the time I spent with her during the storm, I thought and hoped it would lead to something permanent. It never happened. We somehow failed to connect right away, and after a couple of months, I was fairly sure she didn't want us to. I had no idea why, I just had the feeling she didn't.

So why was I so interested in going to Minnesota now, mostly to find her. I pondered the question all the way up Highway 54 to the Kansas Turnpike.

Shortly after I got on it, I stopped and filled the rig and went over to McDonald's for a takeout breakfast sandwich, hash browns, and coffee.

I finished my breakfast before I reached Emporia, where I left the turnpike. I made good time on I35, and it was just after the worst of the rush hour when I drove around Kansas City. I filled the rig as soon as I was around the city.

Heading north out of Kansas City on I35 was a long stretch of freeway I never minded. Even with all the truck traffic, it was still a pretty drive through the rolling hills of Missouri and southern Iowa. At Des Moines, I stopped enjoying it.

I35 and I80 run together there for a while, then split off on the north side of Des Moines. I35 turns off to the left so I had to drive in the left lane for a few miles. I drove the speed limit in the RV, so there was always an angry motorist or trucker about two inches behind me the whole way. That is never fun.

From Des Moines to Minneapolis was mostly flat cornfields and heavy traffic, so all my concentration was on driving in the heavy traffic. I ignored all my other surroundings the whole way.

I filled up again just south of Burnsville so I wouldn't have to think about doing it for a while. The traffic from there to I494 and the rest of the way around Minneapolis and suburbs was its usual miserable self. The Twin Cities has one of the worst, most jammed-up freeway systems I've ever driven. It never mattered where you were or when you were there, the freeways always seemed to be inadequate for the traffic. There were also many sections where there were so many freeways and highways running together, that calling them confusing is an understatement. The only good thing was the fact I'd driven them enough so I didn't get lost.

I drove all the way to Elk River, north of Minneapolis, where there's a decent RV park, before I stopped again. It's often full in the summer, but because it was now September, they had several empty slots.

Once I was settled in, I opened a cold beer, the first one since I left Tucson. It tasted real good while I walked around the RV and car, making sure that nothing had broken or fallen off on the long trip. That's something about driving a RV. You never know what's going to go wrong next.

Back in the RV, I opened second beer and called Bill.

"What the hell are you doing here already?" he asked when I told him where I was. "I figured it'd take you three or four days to get here, driving your RV. I thought they used too much gas if you drove them fast."

"I drove a steady sixty-five most of the way and didn't have any problems or get lost anywhere. I always start every day in the wee small hours, so I made good time. Are you busy tomorrow? I thought we should get together, drink a couple of beers, and tell each other a few lies."

"I'd love to. The thing is, I didn't expect you here yet and I promised Jen I would go up there for the day," he said, referring to his daughter. "I haven't been there for a while and Jen, Pete, and the grandkids really want me to come for a visit."

"That sounds like fun. We can get together in a day or two."

"If it sounds like fun to you, why don't you come along? For me, it's a long drive to Sturgeon Lake alone. I wouldn't at all mind some company. Not to mention, Jen would love to see you and to show off her farm. You and Mary were the ones who got her interested in that way of life you know."

"Hell yes, I'd love to go along. It sounds like a great way to spend a day. I've always wanted to see her place anyway. This will be good time to do it."

"Okay, I'll swing by about eight and pick you up."

"I'm looking forward to it already. And while I have you on the phone, have you heard anything from or about Peri?"

"Last I heard, she flew to San Francisco when she left Tucson. I'll give Judy a call tonight and find out if she knows anything."

"Really, she went to San Francisco. She must be on some kind of mission."

"I guess. I'll let you know tomorrow what I learn from Judy."

After I finished talking to Bill, I decided to call my son. I wasn't at all in the mood, but I knew if I didn't, I'd be listening to more bitching than if I did it now.

"What the hell are you doing up here?" was his first comment when he answered the phone.

"I just decided to come for a visit since there's nothing that needs doing in Tucson."

"It's nothing but a goddamn desert down there anyway, so what could need doing?"

"I only called to let you know I'm here."

"Okay. Gladys and I are busy for the next two or three days. If you're still here when we have some free time, maybe we'll get together then."

"Right," I said and hung up on him. Still in Minnesota or not, there would be no get-together. There was no way I wanted to see him or his wife, Gladys, now. The time comes when enough is enough and this was the time for me.

I never did understand all the reasons he and I couldn't get along. Only some of them. He always hated living on the farm and considered it my fault that we did. It didn't matter that Mary explained many times that the farm was her idea and her dream. She loved gardening and working outside. After she convinced me we should buy the farm, she spent every possible minute every summer working in what started as a garden and soon grew to be fields of vegetables. She was a fourth grade school teacher, so she always had her summers free to do it. I helped as much as I could, but being a carpenter meant that summers were the busiest time of the year for me.

She raised a large variety of vegetables but specialized in peppers and tomatoes. The bulk of her crops were originally the standard tomatoes and green peppers. She also raised a lot of specialty items of both crops. As hot peppers and heirloom tomatoes grew in popularity, she increased the varieties until they were the bulk of what she grew to sell.

She always did well at the farmer's market and made enough money to pay for all the tools and machines we needed for the farm, with enough left over to cover a lot of extras like vacations and entertainment. Because of that, we also managed invest a decent amount during the main part of our working years.

The kid could never accept any of it. As far as he was concerned, I was a slave driver and my forcing his mother work so hard is the reason she died so young. It didn't matter that there was absolutely no truth in it, it was his opinion and he wasn't about to change his mind. Mary having diabetes for fifty years had nothing to do with it as far as he was concerned.

Our relationship got even worse after he graduated from Business College and became a corporate accountant. From then on, he knew everything, and the thing he knew the best was that everything that ever went wrong was my fault. What he didn't know was that I had a real hard time caring about his opinions any longer. The day might come when I would see him again, I wasn't sure. It for sure wouldn't be this trip, or any trip very soon, for that matter. If we ever got together again, he would have to make the effort.

It took me a while before I got over the disgust I felt after my conversation with the kid. It was the memories of my life with Mary and the farm we lived on so many years that gradually replaced it. We had a good life even though we never had the second child we wanted.

When the first one was born, all the doctors told us she should never do it again. With her diabetes, it was too dangerous. Things might have worked out better if we could have had another one, but given the choice between having another child and the possibility of losing Mary, it simply wasn't a choice. I had a vasectomy a couple of months after the kid was born.

CHAPTER 5

After two days in the RV, I definitely needed a walk. I watched the sunrise as I walked around the RV park and down by the river that ran along the west side. No one else was out and about yet, so it was a pleasant walk, even though it was shorter than I felt like I needed.

I cooked and ate breakfast, washed the dirty dishes, and was waiting for Bill, when true to his word, he picked me up just before eight. I threw my bag with the cameras and extra cards and batteries in the back seat of Bill's car, and we immediately left for Sturgeon Lake and his daughter Jen's farm.

"What's in the bag?" Bill asked.

"Cameras and stuff."

"You plan on taking some pictures."

"Probably a lot of them."

Having Bill drive was fine with me. After the long drive the previous two days, it felt good to be able sit back and relax during the ride.

We took Highway 169 north past the towns of Zimmerman, Princeton, Long Siding, and Pease, then picked up Highway 23 in Milaca. It took us to I35, near Hinckley, which we stayed on until the Sturgeon Lake exit.

"It looks like we're going to have a nice day," I said when we started out.

"According to the weather news on TV this morning," Bill said, "it's going to be. It's supposed to be sunshine all day and in the low seventies at Jen's. Here, it'll be closer to eighty."

"Good. It sounds like a perfect Minnesota day."

"I'd think almost any day here would seem like perfect to you since you live where it's hotter than hell all the time."

"No, not really. The heat's never a problem for me. And come winter, the heat in Tucson is wonderful compared to the misery of living through a Minnesota winter."

"I don't mind the winter. It has its good points."

"Really. How come I never noticed any?"

"Probably because you didn't look for them. Winter's a time to rest some after the busy days of summer. It's a good time to stay inside, catch up on reading and fun projects."

"Well, that's your opinion, Bill. I'll take the heat and the lack of snow to shovel. Not to mention, I can hike in the mountains any day of the year. So what have you read lately that's good?"

"To tell you the truth, I haven't been reading much since Nancy died. I can't concentrate on things the way I used to. Mostly I've been wasting my time watching TV when I try to relax, which isn't all that often. Mostly I putter around the house and yard or spend time on the Internet."

"I know what you mean about not being able to concentrate. I've been the same way. You've been alone longer than I have, so I was hoping you were going to be able to tell me how deal with it."

"I wish I could, Ken. For me, my family has been a lot of help. The kids especially. My sister Judy and brother Steve come around some too, and that helps. The only one I haven't seen much of since Nancy died is Peri."

"Yeah, I bet it does help to have your family around. Trouble I have is, I don't have any family in Tucson. My sister Marge lives in Georgia and my brother Carl in California. So what's the deal with Peri?"

"So far as anyone knows, she's either still in San Francisco or on her way to San Diego. I don't know anything more than that." He paused and gave me a curious look when I didn't answer him. "Maybe you ought to think about moving back here, even if you don't like the winters," he said, not commenting on my look of disappointment.

"There's no close family here."

"Your boy's still here, isn't he?"

"We don't get along at all, Bill. One of the blessings of living in Tucson is the fact that there's eighteen hundred miles between us. It's the best way I know of to keep the peace between us."

"Don't you miss your grandkids?"

"I do, but it's hard to get close to them when their father has the attitude he has. I don't know, maybe it is all my fault. I never felt like I was what you'd call a great father, and I think I'm worse at being a grandfather."

"It's too bad you feel that way because you're wrong," Bill said as we started around the town of Princeton. "And I know you'd feel better if you could see him and your grandkids at least once in a while. Don't you kind of miss some of this country around here? You and Mary lived here for a long time."

"Sometimes I miss the summers," I said, remembering when the highway went through Princeton, before they built the highway around it. It was slow going then, especially Friday nights when so many people were on their way for a weekend in northern Minnesota. "Life was good then. It never mattered to Mary or me how hard the work was when Mary was farming, we both loved it."

"Mary did most of the work, didn't she?"

"She did, especially the cultivating, harvesting, and marketing. I always made time in the spring to do the prep work in the fields, and helped as much as I could with the planting. The rest of it, I helped when I could. I always wanted to do more, but being a carpenter, I had to work when the work was there. All in all though, we had a good life. I definitely have nothing to complain about."

"I remember when you guys bought that farm." Bill chuckled. "You weren't sure it was a good idea, were you?"

"No, I wasn't. I was worried about spending that much money on a piece of ground that looked to me like it was near worthless. I wasn't sure we could afford it at the time, either. Letting Mary talk me into it was the smartest thing I ever did. At least with money."

"You did okay when you sold the farm, didn't you?"

"A bit more than okay. Money isn't something I need to worry about now. Mary and I saved some over the years, and with all the development going on up here, we got a hell of a lot more for the farm than I ever thought it would be worth."

"I hope you don't mind my asking, but what's a hell of a lot more than you thought?"

"Pushing seven figures. We bought the hundred and twenty acres for just under two hundred and acre, so we made a hell of a profit on it. The house itself, on just an acre, was worth over two hundred grand. I built it and all the additions on it, as you know, so we didn't have anywhere near that in it. The real estate guy said that if we were willing to wait, he could have got us more than a million for the land. The thing is, at the time, waiting wasn't an option."

"Mary wasn't doing very good by then, was she?"

"No, and once we knew we had to sell out, it was a lot easier to just let it go. Trying to hang on to it would have been too painful for Mary. As far as I was concerned at the time and now too, Mary was more important than money."

"That makes sense. When you live with someone as long as you two were together, nothing else does."

"That's right. I'm sure you felt the same way about Nancy."

"Of course I did. We just didn't have time to plan what happened. With Nancy, she was fine one day, the next day she was dead."

"It had to have been hard, losing her that way."

"It was. Losing someone you love is always hard. No matter how it happens. At least I knew there was a chance that something could go wrong when she decided to have surgery on her cataracts. Taking her off the coumadin, which is a blood thinner as you know, was a gamble. Especially after all the years she was on it. There was no way to know if she would have another blood clot. I wasn't so sure she should do it, but for Nancy, it was an easy decision. There was no way she wanted to go blind."

"Life's a bitch when you're forced to make those kind of choices."

"It is, but at least she didn't suffer. When that blood clot hit her brain, she was gone almost instantly."

Our conversation was getting a little depressing, so we rode quiet for a while. I watched the scenery until enough time passed to start talking about something different.

"You said you spend a lot of time on the Internet, Bill," I said. "What do you do on the Internet?"

"Mostly I browse around, reading political stuff. It's interesting, reading the total shit that those conservatives write. Especially the right-wing evangelical Christians. Talk about a bunch of idiots."

"I mostly try to avoid listening to anything they say or reading what they write. Mostly, I try to avoid anything at all about them. They make me crazy. All conservatives make me crazy. They're so damn seldom right, no matter what the subject."

"You are absolutely correct. All they want to do is keep lowering the taxes on the rich, raising taxes on the rest of us, and start totally stupid wars so they can wave the flag and pretend that they're patriotic and heroic."

"The sad part of it is, most people buy into their bullshit. Why do people worry about crap like abortion when it's not the governments business in the first place? The right wingers don't even want people to have access to birth control. You have to be a moron not to know that plant earth already is overcrowded with people."

"Yeah, I know. Homosexuals all ought to be persecuted and never given equal rights. There's no such thing as global warming, 'cause only God can do that, and pollution isn't a problem. What we need is more growth. Screw the environment and everything else that really matters."

"You know, Bill, we could both go on and on with all these subjects. I just don't think we'll ever disagree on any of them."

"You're right, it's not likely we would."

"Except one. Your ex-brother-in-law, Don Gray. He was one of them. I don't know how you stood that asshole."

"Are you saying that because he was married to Peri, or do you have some better reasons?"

"I've got a lot of reasons. He constantly preached about all the things we just talked about and always took the opposite side. He always acted and talked as if he was a genius and the rest of us were idiots."

"I know, but he wasn't that bad a guy. He just had different beliefs than we do."

"That's fine. He was still an asshole. Especially what he did to Peri."

"He was always good to her. He was patient and never hurt her."

"The hell he didn't. What about her breast cancer?"

"Well, I guess you've got a point there. He was just following his faith though."

"Bullshit! When he got sick, he went to the doctor. She gets a lump in her breast, and he tells her all she has to do is wear a crystal around her neck and pray harder. Going to a doctor for it would be a sin. How long did she have that lump before she finally went to the doctor?"

"About a year."

"And why did she finally go?"

"Because I found out about it and made her go."

"What more do I have to say? Don Gray was an asshole, an idiot, and if I would've known where he was when I found out what he did, I might have killed him."

"At least she made a full recovery."

"There's still no excuse for what he did, faith or not. People like him are supposed to be so damn wonderful, just because they're so full of righteousness. The only thing they have is self-righteousness. Them and that Bible they're always quoting. A hell of a lot of the problems with the environment will never be solved, all because of the book of Genesis. The Devil's Handbook would be a better title for it."

"You always seemed to get along with him though."

"I was trying to be nice. It didn't make any sense to not get along with him. That doesn't mean I ever agreed with him or liked him. And I sure as hell never respected the stupid son-of-a-bitch."

"To tell you the truth, Ken, I didn't like him that much either. He was Peri's husband, so I overlooked a lot."

"At least he died young and she's finally rid of him."

"Yes, she is. Now I have a question that I hope you don't mind my asking. What is it with you and Peri?"

"What do you mean?"

"Exactly what I asked. It's always been obvious that there's been something between you two."

"I'm not sure what you mean by something between us," I said, not wanting to answer his question.

"Sure you do. For as long as I can remember, you two have had something going on. I'm just wondering about it."

"The only thing I can say is that she's always been special to me. Even when we were kids."

"Like that summer you and her spent all your time together?"

"It started before that, Bill. Long before that. It started when I met her. I was five years old. Ever since then, I've always had a special place inside for her. That summer we were together all the time was really special. To this day, I wish it could have lasted. If not forever, at least a lot longer."

"I figured it was like that."

"It is like that. It always has been."

"And that's why you came to Minnesota to find her?"

"I wanted to come for a visit anyway. Finding her is the reason I finally decided to make the trip."

"Well, I hope she shows up before you have to go back to Tucson, after coming this far to see her."

"So do I, but coming back to Minnesota is something I needed to do. I always enjoy getting together with you too. I miss having someone my age to talk to, who has a brain."

"I feel the same way about you. The kids are great, but there's always a bit of a generation gap. It's no one's fault, it's just there. Most other people just aren't interested in much more than what it takes to get by or their day-to-day lives."

"I know, most of the time when I try to talk about any of the things you and I talk about all the time, I either bore people or piss them off."

Bill laughed. "That's about it."

We were quiet again for a while. I watched the scenery as we rolled down I35 at a steady seventy. The freeway was straight, the land was flat, and most of the time, pine trees lined both sides of the road, with occasional breaks where a farmer's fields were open to it. It's pretty country, yet obvious, as it was since we went around Princeton, that no one is ever going to get rich farming in Northern Minnesota.

Mary and I did well when we farmed, mostly because we never had to make a living at it. Farming was Mary's passion, and as much as she liked teaching, I'm sure if it was possible to make a living at it, farming would have been her fulltime occupation.

"You sure got quiet all the sudden," Bill said finally.

"Sorry about that. I was thinking about how difficult it must be for the farmers in this area. I don't see how they could be making much of a living farming around here."

"I doubt that most of them are. Jen and Pete don't even try. They pretty much do it the way you and Mary did. It's a sideline. One that pays them well but never enough to live on."

"Pete makes enough so Jen doesn't have to work, doesn't he?"

"Yes, he makes a damn good living doing the cable work. He's gotten to the point now that he does most of the technical work on whatever job he's on."

"Does he still travel around most of the time?"

"He does. This year isn't as bad as most. He's been in South Dakota all year, so Jen has spent a lot of time with him."

"What do they do with the boys when she's gone?"

"Nothing. They stay home and take care of themselves."

"They must be damn good kids, if she can leave them alone that way."

"They are. They've never had a problem leaving them. Jen brought them up right, and both boys are very self-sufficient. Home schooling them had a lot to do with it too. There's a lot less bad influence from their peers that way."

"That would be a help."

"You'll be able to see for yourself what kind of kids they are shortly. The next exit is for Sturgeon Lake. Their farm is only a little over five miles from there."

My feelings were mixed as we got closer to their farm. Even though I'd never seen it, I knew it was going to bring up a lot of memories. Mary was much on my mind when we turned into their driveway.

CHAPTER 6

Jen and Pete's farm carried the look and feel of the farm Mary and I owned, yet there were a lot of distinct differences. Their house was near a hundred years old, but the remodeling Pete did since they bought it was obvious. It was now an up-to-date beautiful home. Scattered all around were a couple of pole buildings and a lot of small buildings, all constructed in recent years.

Some were used for the animals they raised, others the use wasn't readily obvious.

When Mary and I bought our farm, it was bare land, with no buildings of any kind. With a lot of help from friends, we built every building that was on the place when we sold it.

I worked with and around a lot of great guys all the years I was a carpenter, and all of us helped each other out when anyone had a building project. I spent fair amount of weekends working on projects with most of them, be it a deck, room addition, finishing a basement, a reproofing job, or any number of other things. I always made it a point to not accept payment of any kind, other than party time at the end of the day, for doing it.

When it came time for me to build our house, we got a lot of free help. I drew the print for the small, two-bedroom, one-bath, ranch-style house we started with. Mary's parents borrowed us the money for the materials so we could avoid the cost of a construction loan. We secured a mortgage from the local bank in Princeton, something that would be impossible now in the age of big corporate banks. So it was it was a lot simpler process to build it than it would be now.

The Saturday we started construction, the basement walls and footings were in. A lot of the guys showed up to help, and by the end of the day, we had all the walls up and sheeted, the trusses were set, the roof was sheeted, the fascia and soffits were installed, and the roof was covered with felt.

By the end of the second Saturday, the shingles were on the roof, all the exterior windows and doors were installed, and the siding was nailed on.

I hired a couple of friends to do the plumbing and wiring, following the principle of doing what you do best and paying for the rest. Then I installed the insulation, and four of us finished the drywall on a Saturday. I was smart enough to hire another friend to do the drywall taping, which is a skill that takes years to develop. Mary and I painted it ourselves, inside and out, and four of us installed the kitchen and trimmed the inside on a weekend.

About a month after we moved in and got more or less settled, we threw a big party for everyone who helped build the house. A few other friends came too, treating the occasion like a house warming: Bill and Nancy and Peri and her husband Don, along with some of Mary's friends from the Princeton school system.

Mary was a wizard in the kitchen, and with my help with the mundane preparations, we put together a ten-course meal. She liked to cook a lot of different foods, so that if anyone didn't like one type, sooner or later, they'd find something they did like. We started the party in the afternoon and served the food one course at a time, about an hour apart, as the day and evening wore on. She started the meal with three courses: egg foo young, fried rice, and egg rolls. After that it was chili, clam chowder, Italian spaghetti, meatballs, roast pork with mashed potatoes and gravy, a large tossed salad, and finished it with a huge platter of fried chicken.

Everyone was having a good time and enjoying the food, so even though the beer and wine was flowing freely, no one got drunk. It was late before people started leaving. Mary and Nancy did a lot of the cleanup as the evening wore on, but there was still a fair amount to do at the end.

Mary, Nancy, and Peri were finishing up in the kitchen when the crowd was gone, Bill and Don were napping on each end of the couch, so I went outside to listen to the summer night sounds. The temperature was down into the seventies, it was late enough for almost all of the evening mosquitoes to be gone, so it was very pleasant outside.

I was tired but happy about the way the party had gone and was lost in my thoughts when suddenly someone was standing close to my side. Peri surprised me when she leaned against me, then surprised me even more when she took my hand and squeezed it.

"Hi," she said, "you looked kind of lonesome out here all by yourself."

"No, not lonesome. Just enjoying the night air and the sounds of all the critters out there in the woods and swamps."

"Oh, does that mean you're not glad to see me?"

"I'm always happy to see you, Peri. Did you enjoy the party?"

"Sure. I'd have liked it better if I spent more of it with you."

"I was here the whole time."

"Sure you were, just not with me." She turned to face me, put her hand around the back of my neck, and pulled me down to kiss me.

I don't know if she intended to do more than give me a light kiss. It quickly turned into a lot more. When we finally paused to catch our breath, she took my hand and put it on her breast.

"That's so you don't forget who I am next time." She smiled, kissed me again, gave my hand another squeeze, and went back inside.

I stayed outside until everyone was ready to leave. After they were gone and Mary and I were getting ready to go to bed, Mary said, "Peri has really got something for you."

"What? What are you talking about?"

"I'm talking about you and Peri. There's something between the two of you."

"Well, even if there was once, it's nothing for you to worry about. That's all over and has been for a long time. I love you, Mary, and I'll never let anything or anyone change that. You're way too important to me. I plan to spend the rest of my life with you, so don't be trying to get rid of me."

Mary gave me a hug, smiled, and said, "That's the last thing I'm trying to do, Ken. I just want you to know that I know there's something between you two, and I think it's probably something special. I can see it in her eyes every time she looks at you. I also want you to know that I'm not worried about it, as long as you never let it come between you and me."

"Don't worry, I won't. No way do I ever want to mess up what you and I have."

"Good. There's one more thing I want you to know. If you stick to that, when something does happen between the two of you, and I'm sure it will eventually, as long as you don't let it screw up what we have, I think it will be okay."

"Mary, I—"

"Enough said. Let's go to bed. Tonight you're mine."

I was, and she reminded me, as she always did when I needed to be reminded, why I loved her and never wanted to lose her.

"We're here," Bill said, poking me in the shoulder.

"Yeah, I know."

"Well, you sure as hell could have fooled me," he said with a chuckle, "you went off into never-never land for a while there. I thought maybe you were asleep."

"No, just remembering. Seeing this farm brought up a lot of remembering."

"I can see why it would do that. Even this far north, this place is a lot like your farm."

Jen was out of the house to greet us as soon as we got out of the car. She gave Bill a big hug first, then I got mine.

"It's good to see you, Ken," she smiled, "it's been a few years."

"It has," I agreed. "I haven't seen you since Mary and I moved to Tucson. Now, are you going to show me around? This is the first time I've been here."

"Of course. Pete and the boys are working out in the woods, so I'll take you out there first."

"Are they putting up firewood?"

"No, they're taking down a couple of big oaks. Pete bought a small mill and he's anxious to try it out."

"Are you going to be selling the wood?"

"Maybe some, but we've got more building projects in mind, and the boys will be using a lot of it in as soon as it's dry enough."

I took my cameras out of the car, and we followed Jen out to the woods. It was a dry summer so far, so the mosquitoes weren't as bad as they are some years.

We also had a light breeze, which helped, and I did my best to ignore the rest of them as I walked, constantly snapping pictures.

We started the walk going through a large pasture where four head of beef cattle grazed contentedly in the tall, if somewhat dry grass. Two head were full grown, and the other two were yearlings.

"Are you going to have the cattle butchered, or are you going to ship them?" I asked Jen.

"Pete's going to butcher one in a couple of weeks. The other one will depend on deer season. If we get enough venison, we'll ship one. If not, it'll get butchered this winter. We'll do the young stock next year."

"Pete does his own butchering?"

"Of course. There's no sense in paying someone else for doing it. He butchers all the animals and makes and smokes the sausage, bacon, and hams."

"You're doing a lot more than Mary and I did. Early on, I butchered chickens, ducks, and geese, but after a while, I couldn't do it. It seemed like I was killing our pets. So we gave up trying to raise them, which was fine with Mary, since she didn't eat a lot of meat. We did put up a lot of fruit and vegetables though, both canning and freezing, every year except the last one on the farm. By then, we knew we were going to sell out, so it didn't make any sense to do it."

"No, I guess it wouldn't."

After we left the pasture, we crossed some low ground, which looked as though it was normally wet. It was dry now. From there, we followed a narrow farm road deep into the woods.

Pete and the boys had already cut two trees down. Pete and Kyle, the oldest boy, were trimming the branches off a huge oak with chainsaws. Lee, the younger of the boys, was wrapping a heavy chain around the other tree, which was already trimmed. After that, he connected the chain to a large John Deere tractor, so they could drag the tree out of the woods.

I took pictures of the work in progress, and Bill and Jen stood there waiting until the tree trimming was completed. As soon as the chainsaws were stopped, Pete gave us a big grin and me a hearty handshake.

"It's good to see you again, Ken. Glad you could come. You going to be in Minnesota long?"

"I don't know. I don't have any definite plans. A few days ago, a trip to Minnesota wasn't something I had any plans for."

"Really? Well, I'm glad you decided to come. Jen's been hoping you would since we bought this place. She wanted you to see it, more than anyone else. Ever since she spent part of that summer with you and Mary when she was a kid, having a farm like this has been her dream."

I appreciated the fact that he didn't tell me how nice it would be if Mary could see their farm too. I already knew it, but the less I had to talk about it, the better. The empty hole she left inside me when she died was big enough already.

As soon as Pete and the boys moved the branches from the second oak into the pile of tree trimmings they'd started, Kyle climbed onto the John Deere, started it, pulled the chain up tight, and dragged it home. The powerful tractor pulled the tree as if there was nothing there.

The rest of us walked behind. I took a lot of pictures of everyone and everything else that looked interesting, so we didn't talk much.

Jen took me on a tour of the house as soon as we got back. It was obvious right away that they did a great job with their remodeling. Throughout they maintained the look and feel of an old farmhouse, and even the new modern kitchen they put in didn't detract from it. The appliances were all designed to appear ancient, and the cooking stove used either LP gas or wood, and even though it was new, it looked older than the house. Some of the furniture were antiques and the rest well-done replicas.

"You guys did a great job with this," I told Jen. "Even the antique replicas are really well done."

"Pete and the boys built most of them, and almost everything else, we bought at auctions and yard sales."

"However you did it, you did a great job."

"Maybe you don't remember, Ken, but you had a lot to do with this. You helped Pete a lot with the way you answered his questions when he was starting to build things. He's always said you were a lot of help."

"I remember answering a few questions, I just never thought I was much help."

"You were."

After we toured the house, we went outside to look through the collection of small buildings Pete and the boys built. She showed me her building first. It was her sewing center. Inside, she had about fifteen machines, from an old Singer treadle, to a computerized machine with more dials, buttons, and do-dads than I would have thought possible.

Pete's building was a fully equipped machine shop and garage. It was loaded with mechanic's tools, welders, a metal lathe, a cutting torch, and a grease pit. Lee's building was a fully equipped woodworking shop, and the projects he was building were incredible. Especially for someone only fifteen.

Everything from dressers, to patio furniture, to intricate boxes loaded with drawers and compartments.

Kyle's building was primarily used for woodcarving and was dominated by a large workbench. He also had a small table saw, a miter saw, and a wood lathe. All of his tools and carving chisels were impressive, but his carvings on display were more impressive than anything I'd seen.

While we were inside, he showed me what he was working on. It was a wood elf he was carving out of bark. His hands moved fast as the elf rapidly took shape in the bark.

"How can you visualize that ahead of time?" I asked.

"It's easy," he explained. "The woods and trees are full of elves. All you have to do is look at a piece of bark or wood for a while, and you can see them. Then it's just a matter of cutting out the wood in the way, and there they are."

Seventeen years old, and he was doing the work I would've expected from someone my age that carved their whole life. The kid wasn't just a craftsman, he was an artist or maybe a genius. I was a reasonably good carpenter and woodworker, but compared to Kyle, my work was no more than ordinary.

"You've got to be proud of this family of yours," I told Bill. "They sure as hell are a talented bunch."

"I am," he said, grinning. "Who would've ever thought there'd be any artists in my family?"

Jen took us out to see her large garden, already slightly frostbitten, which was no big surprise that far north in Minnesota. Then we visited the pigs, the chickens, and the rabbits they raised for meat.

Pete had hamburgers on the grill when we finished the tour, and Jen gave us each a beer as we waited for the food to get done.

"I'm very much impressed with your farm," I told her. "And those boys of yours sure do some awesome work. As good as they are already, by the time they get to be my age, they probably be famous."

"I don't know about that, but I think they're good enough to make a living at it eventually."

"I don't think there's any doubt about that."

Pete finished the hamburgers and Jen brought out a large bowl of salad. We ate the burgers on homemade buns with thick slices of red onions from the garden and the salad with homemade blue cheese dressing.

"So," Pete asked as we ate, "what made you suddenly decide to visit Minnesota?"

"It's something I've thought about doing off and on for a while, but this time…" I told them about the call for Peri and how I missed her that day by a couple of minutes.

"So you came up here because you wanted to see her?"

"To find her, and yes, hopefully to see her."

"I hate to tell you this, Ken," Jen said, "but unless you plan on staying here for a while, you probably won't. I talked to her on the phone last night. She's still in San Diego, and she said she'd be there for a few more days. When she leaves there, she's going to Gainesville, Georgia."

"No kidding? My sister lives there."

"That's right. As a matter of fact, she said she's going to stay with your sister while she's there. I didn't even make the connection until just now."

It was a surprise to hear Peri was going to stay with Marge. I didn't think they were that close. Then again, they were the same age and did grow up together.

"Do you know why Peri's traveling all over," I asked, "the way she is?"

"Didn't Dad tell you?" Jen gave Bill a curious look.

"I didn't tell him, Jen," Bill said, "because I don't know either. I haven't seen or talked to her for quite a while."

"Is there something Bill and I should know, Jen?" I asked.

"I…well, I'm not sure." She bit her lower lip, making it obvious there was.

It was easy to see she didn't think she should say anything more, so I let it drop. I knew already that I was going to Georgia. If I were lucky enough to find Peri there, maybe she would tell me.

CHAPTER 7

Kyle and Lee took me out in the woods again that afternoon. They said they wanted me to see more of it while I was there, but I also suspect they were testing me, to see if an old man like me could handle good hike.

We covered some fairly rough ground and went through some thick brush, but with all the hiking I always did, it wasn't difficult. The only problem I had was the pace they set. I normally didn't walk as fast as they did. I think they were satisfied with my performance anyway.

Later that afternoon, while we were all relaxing in lawn chairs, Pete asked me, "Why did you and Mary move to Tucson? It seems like kind of a strange place to live after all your years on a farm in Minnesota."

"Mary loved Tucson. She went down there every year with her folks. They started going when she was pretty young. While she was in college and then teaching, they always went during spring break. The only time she didn't go is when she was pregnant and the kid's first year. After that, she always took him along."

"Didn't you ever go?"

"I did the first couple of years we were married. After Mary got the farm going, I stayed home. The greenhouse was always full of plants she was starting for the fields and garden. They needed regular watering, and even though the heating system was decent, I kept an eye on it. One cold spring night with the heat off, and we would likely lose everything. Tomatoes and peppers especially, won't take much cold. None of the other plants could have taken a hard freeze either."

"That makes sense. Did you like Tucson?"

"I love it, and don't ever plan to leave. I think I'm a real desert rat at heart, and I love hiking in the mountains. The only thing I miss is people like you guys and Bill."

"Why didn't you and Mary move down there sooner, if it suits you so well?"

"She loved farming more. If she would have stayed healthy, I'm sure we'd still be on the farm."

"It sounds like you enjoyed the farm too, if you stayed home like that while she went to Tucson."

"I did. It was a good life. Staying home to take care of things wasn't a burden."

Except for the burden of a big guilt trip more than once, I thought. *Thanks to Peri.*

A hard rain woke me up around six in the morning, the first time it happened. I dragged myself out of bed, and after pouring myself a cup of hot coffee, I wandered into the living room. I checked the thermometer outside the window. It was a meager thirty-five degrees.

The rain continued to come down hard, so I wasn't surprised when the boss called to tell me were laying off for the day. I was working with a framing crew, and there wasn't much we could get done on a day like that.

It was mid-morning and I was out in the greenhouse watering when she got there.

"I thought you weren't home until I noticed your truck," she said when she joined me in the greenhouse, soaking wet. "When you didn't answer the door, I thought you might be out here."

"This is a surprise," I said. "I haven't seen you for quite a while, Peri. What brings you here on a miserable day like this?"

"Oh, Don's gone this week and I didn't feel like going to work. I called in sick today. I got bored sitting around the house, so I decided to go for a ride in the rain. And here I am. Standing in a greenhouse, dripping wet and cold, and talking to you."

"Just give me a couple of minutes and we'll go in the house and find something dry for you to wear. We can throw those clothes in the drier."

"Good. You know, I didn't really expect to find you home. I decided to stop anyway. I knew there'd be a chance you'd be here if you were doing your carpenter work outside right now."

"That's what I've been doing for a while. So where's Don?"

"He's at one of his religious seminars this week. It's in Madison, Wisconsin this time."

"What does he, or anyone for that matter, do at a religious seminar?"

"Oh, he sits around with a bunch of other preacher types and they talk about God, study the Bible, and try to figure better ways to make money preaching."

"Why didn't you go with him? I thought you were really into the religious thing."

"If you don't mind, Ken, I'd rather not get into religion right now. I believe what I believe. So let's leave it at that. I didn't go with Don because what he's doing right now bores the hell out of me."

"Okay. I didn't mean to upset you."

"You didn't. What time does Mary get home?"

"She's in Tucson. Don't you remember? She goes down there every year with her folks during spring break."

"Oh, that's right. I forgot." Peri did a lousy job of hiding her smile.

I finished the watering, and we went in the house. I found one of Mary's bathrobes for her and showed her the bathroom, even though she knew where it was.

"You can take off your wet clothes in here and wear this while they dry."

When she came out of the bathroom wearing the robe, she hadn't tied it as tight as she could have. I tried hard to pretend to not notice how much she was displaying on top, even though it looked very inviting.

"How's life been treating you, Ken?" she asked after she relaxed in the lounge chair in the living room across from me on the couch.

"Good, life's been good. I damn sure don't have anything to complain about."

It was hard while I talked to her, to keep my eyes where they belonged. She let the bathrobe flop open on her legs, all the way to her thighs. It wasn't hard to know that she was doing a number on me. The question was, what was she really after? I figured she was just giving me a hard time or, at the most, trying to tease some. Her flirting or teasing wouldn't be a first.

For a long time, she'd been doing it every chance she got. I didn't think she ever did it to be mean or nasty. It seemed more like it was her special way of relating to me. I never saw her do it to anyone else. Either way, we always seemed to have a special kind of friendship.

"Can I get you some coffee or something, Peri?"

"No, I'm fine."

She dropped down the footrest on the chair and leaned forward, making no attempt to close the robe when it flopped open enough to show me her breasts almost to her nipples.

"Do I look like I'm getting old to you, Ken? I'm over thirty now, so maybe I am starting to look old."

"Hell no, why did you ask me that?"

"It's the way your eyes keep moving around, like you don't want to look at me."

"I think you know the reasons for my not looking. Your being or getting old doesn't have anything to do with it. It's the exact opposite and we both know it."

"Then why are you trying so hard?"

"You're married, I'm married. If I look at what you're showing me right now, I'll want to take advantage of you. I don't really want to do that. You're my friend and I want to keep you as friend."

"Damn you, Ken. You are always such a straight arrow. Do the right thing. It's no wonder I've never felt good enough for you."

"That's about as far from the truth as anything could ever get. Not good enough for me. I have no idea why you would ever believe that. Too good for me is more accurate."

"Why, Ken, did you ever get such a goofy idea?"

"Because for a lot of years, I wanted us to get together. When we were young, I always hoped you and I would get married. The fact that it never happened always seemed to be your choice, not mine."

"It was, just not for the reasons you think. I never wanted to hurt you. I was always sure that if you and I ever made anything permanent, I would. I just knew I would somehow screw it up."

"And now?"

"Now, as you well know, it's too late. All you and I can ever have now are moments. Most of them very small moments. But sometimes, on days like today, maybe those moments can be a little bigger."

"And the people we might hurt?"

"We won't hurt anyone if no one knows. You try to be honest all the time. Not telling anyone anything isn't really being dishonest. It's just like, well, don't bring it up and you won't have to lie about it."

And with that, she got up and sat in my lap. I kissed her and let my hands decide where they wanted to be while Peri worked on the buttons of my shirt. It wasn't until much later that we went to bed.

Peri stayed all day and then stayed the night. We woke up early to bright sunshine, so I knew I was going to be late for work. Peri left right away. I kissed her goodbye, and just before she went out the door, she took my hand and gave it a light squeeze. I spent the day slopping around a very muddy construction site. It was a long one.

When Mary came home, she asked me how the week had gone. I told her fine.

"Did you have any company?"

"Yes," I answered, wondering how she knew, then told her about Peri coming, getting wet walking out to the greenhouse, and using Mary's robe while her clothes dried. "It was a total surprise, Mary. I never expected to see her."

"I thought you must have had someone here, Ken. I never hang anything up the way you hung my bathrobe. Well, it didn't hurt anything. I hope you two had a nice visit." She laughed softly.

Mary never said another word about it nor did she ever again ask me if I had company while she was gone.

Peri didn't visit the next year. Two years later, she did, and then made three more visits over the years. They stopped after she had breast cancer. The times we'd seen each other since then were rare. And always, it was when other people were around. She still flirted and teased on occasion. It just wasn't ever quite the same. It was a long time ago. So why was I trying so hard to find her now?

"Do you want another beer?" Bill asked, rather loud.

"Oh, yeah, sure."

Jen brought me the beer. "You've been awful quiet," she said as she handed it to me.

"I'm sorry, I just got lost in the past for a bit."

"Were you thinking about Peri?"

"Mostly. Mary too. I love this place you and Pete have here. You two have found a good way to live. Mary and I did a lot to be self-sufficient, but we never managed to do as much as you're doing."

"A lot of people think we're crazy." Jen turned to Pete. "Isn't that right?"

"It sure is," he said. "We don't care. We live life the way we want to, and anyone who doesn't like it, it's their problem."

"There's no problem with me, Pete. I admire what you're doing. You've got a couple of great kids too. I've sure had fun with them today."

"Well, thank you. We think they're good kids too. So what are you going to now, Ken? Are you going to stay here for a while or head back to Tucson?"

"I'm going to stay here in Minnesota for a few more days, maybe visit some relatives I haven't seen for a while. After that, I'm not sure. Going to Georgia next is a definite possibility."

"Are you going to go down there to see Peri?" Jen asked.

"It would be nice if I did see her. The way things are going though, I don't think my odds of finding her there are very good. She'll probably be in Alaska or New York or God knows where when I get there. I'd like to visit my sister too. Georgia is closer to Minnesota than Arizona, so I think now would be a good time to go."

"What will you do if you do find Peri there and she doesn't want to see you?"

"Not see her then. All she'll have to do is tell me. I certainly don't want to do anything to bug her or upset her. But after all, she did stop to see me when she was in Tucson. If she hadn't, I probably wouldn't be here right now."

"I didn't mean it quite that way. It's just that she has some things to do she'd rather not have to explain. If you had seen her in Tucson, there wouldn't have been time for her to explain. If you find her in Georgia, there probably will be."

"I'll remember that, and if I do see her, I'll be nice and not ask her any questions."

"What is it with you and Peri?" Pete asked. "It's a bit curious, you trying to find her the way you are."

"That's a big question, Pete. Someday I'll tell you. Some of it anyway. For now, let's just say that Peri and I go way back and leave it go."

"We all go way back," Bill said. "Ken and I have been friends since we were five, and that's a lot of years. When we were kids, we lived in a real neighborhood. A place where kids could play together outside without needing parents watching over them every minute the way it is now. All of us got pretty close back then."

"I'm glad you explained it, Bill. Peri's flying all over the country for some reason only Jen knows. Ken's on a mission to find Peri, so he's driving all around the country hoping he will. And it's all because you guys grew up together in a safe neighborhood. Makes sense."

Bill laughed. "Part of it makes sense, Pete, and that's Jen knowing what's going on with Peri. She's the one who always stays in touch with everyone, so she's the one who always knows what's going on. If I'd of thought of that in the first place, I could've saved Ken the trip up here to Minnesota. He could've gone straight to Georgia."

"I'm glad you didn't, Bill. If you had, I wouldn't be here right now, and I'm very happy to be here. No matter what, there's no place else I'd rather be right now."

"That's a nice thing to say," Jen said.

"It's true. Next time I'm here in the RV, I'd like to come up here and park it for a few days. If you guys wouldn't mind, that is?"

"You're always welcome any time," Pete said. "You can come and stay as long as you want."

"I appreciate that. I'll be looking forward to it."

"Good, and make it sooner rather than later."

"So where are the boys?"

"In their shops, working on their projects."

"I think I'll see what they're up to."

I wanted to do more than see what they were doing. I looked in on Kyle first and picked out one of the wood elves he had hanging on the wall. I thought it would make a nice gift for Marge when I got to Georgia. The kid had the prices marked on the bottom of all of his work. He tried to give me a discount on it. I knew the price was already too low for the quality of his work, so I wouldn't let him.

Lee tried to do the same thing when I bought a black walnut pen he made on the lathe and the gold-plated letter opener with a hand-carved handle I bought for Marge's husband Walt. I wouldn't let him give me a discount either.

I did enough woodworking in my life to know that both of those boys did better work than me, and I was fairly good at it.

Bill was ready to leave when I finished with the boys. I shook hands with Pete, and Jen gave me a big hug. I knew when we left their driveway, that if I never did anything in Minnesota again, this was one place I needed to return to.

CHAPTER 8

Dark shadows covered the country roads has Bill navigated his way to the freeway, so we didn't talk until we were on it. He was the first to speak.

"So you're going to Georgia, Ken?"

"I am. Do you want to ride along?"

"No, I'm not much for traveling. Jen's is about as far as I like to go. I don't even go any farther than that to go fishing or deer hunting."

"You mean you don't want to go down there and be among all those good Christians and conservative Republicans?"

"You said before when you talked about Georgia, that the people down there were really nice."

"They are. They're always friendly no matter where you are. But, and this is a big but, they are some of the most ignorant people I've ever met. You don't have to read much in a newspaper, especially the editorials, to understand why we fought the civil war."

"I kind of figured that. The way they vote down there tells the story. It's the same thing we talked about earlier today. Evangelical Christians and conservatives who know it all. Which would be okay if they weren't so damn ignorant."

"Yeah, and we could go on forever about them, especially if we had something to disagree about. I'm glad we don't. I love to talk, I just hate arguing."

"You've always been like that. Nancy and I never argued much either. How about you and Mary?"

"Very rarely."

And we hadn't. Most of the time I let her make the decisions. She handled our finances, and I never questioned her decisions or how she spent the money. The only time I spent any was when I needed a tool for my job or the woodshop. When I did, I told her what it was for so she could record it in her ledger for tax purposes. Usually, the only time I took the lead in our lives was in bed. Mary rarely did yet never really protested when I did.

The one time she did was shortly after we bought the farm. We made the purchase in late summer, knowing it would be the following spring before we built the house. Often though, we would go there on a weekend day to walk around, explore, and talk about where the house and fields were going to be.

It was on a beautiful day early in October, with the temperature in the mid-seventies. The leaves on the maples and oaks were at their peak of color, filled with brilliant yellows, reds, and scarlet.

Because it was such a nice day, we brought a picnic lunch and a blanket along to sit on. We walked back through the open fields to a huge stand of pines someone planted during the dust bowl time in the thirties.

Mary spread the blanket out when we decided to eat, and as she did, I could see inside her light blouse. Not much, just enough to notice she wasn't wearing a bra. It was something she rarely did outside of the house. She didn't much like them, she just didn't think it was proper to go to out if she wasn't wearing one. This time, it had an instant effect on me. I let her finish with the blanket and sit down. Before she could take the food out, I sat down close to her. I kissed her and pulled her down on the blanket.

"Now what do you think you're doing, Ken? If it's what I think, you'll have to wait until tonight. We can't do it here."

"And why not?"

"What if someone sees us?"

"No one is going to see us way the hell back here. Even if they did, what's the difference?"

"The difference is, it would bother me."

"Let's move the blanket then. There's a lot of room under the pine trees. There's no way anyone will see us there."

"Maybe I don't want to."

"I guess if you really don't want to, I won't push it. It's your fault that I want to though."

"Why is it my fault? I didn't do anything."

"Oh yes, you did. You grew up beautiful and came here with me looking as sexy as a woman can look. Then you bent over and I could see down your blouse."

"You've seen down my blouse before. Many times."

"Yes, I have, and every time I do, you have the same effect on me."

"I guess I should be happy about that. Do you really think no one can see us under those trees?"

"I know they can't."

"You're sure?"

"I am."

Mary moved the blanket onto a soft bed of pine needles under the trees. I took my time then, doing everything I could to get her in the mood. When the time came, she was more than ready, and after, she didn't rush either of us to get dressed.

After we ate and spent a couple of hours walking around and talking about all our plans for the place, we went back to the pine trees to pick up the blanket and the basket we brought the lunch in. Mary started folding the blanket, then smiled, and took the blanket under the trees again.

Another time, I was sure she would argue was a Saturday morning, not long after we moved into our new house. Because I was a carpenter, I always took my shower at night to get rid of the day's sawdust and dirt. Mary took hers in the morning. She was out of bed before I was, so even though I was very much in the mood, I didn't get the chance to try anything.

When I heard the shower, I thought I might as well test her reaction. All she could do is say no.

"What are you doing in here?" she asked when I stepped into the shower.

"I thought I'd wash your back for you."

"Oh, sure," she smiled. "You liar." She took me in her hand. "It's not *hard* to see why you're here."

It was a great way to start a weekend.

"It's too bad, isn't it, Bill," I said as I shook off those good memories, "that Nancy and Mary didn't get the chance to share more of this time of our life. Getting old isn't the greatest, but I pretty much like not going to work unless I want to."

"You're right there. We're both damn lucky to be in this position. It's hard a lot of the time, not having Nancy with me, yet I still consider myself lucky for not having to worry about money."

"Do you have enough put away between now and social security?"

"I have enough. The house is paid for, it has been for a long time, I have my pension, and there was some life insurance on Nancy. As long as I'm careful, I'm going to be just fine."

"How about health insurance? That sure is a mess. The so-called insurance companies are screwing everyone. We had good coverage for Mary that she had while she was teaching and it still covers me. It damn sure ain't cheap though."

"Nor is mine, but at least I'm covered."

"Well, maybe someday, we'll be able to buy insurance provided by the government. If it was set up somewhat like Medicare, it would work a lot better than what the money-grubbing insurance companies provide."

"It surely would do that. I just don't look for it to happen. Most people are conservatives, so they think that would be socialism. And the political and business leaders in this country are going to continue to ram their crap down everyone's throat. God forbid anything should ever be done to cut into the obscene profits of the drug and insurance companies."

"You're right. Most people are too ignorant to understand what those people are doing. There's just not enough of us liberals left to get anything positive done."

"I don't think there will ever be enough of us. Not in our lifetime. The rich own the media, and theirs is the only message that's really getting across. Fairness and human decency isn't part of the message. The politics of hate is what they're selling, and hate sells well."

"It always has."

"So what are your plans if you don't find Peri in Georgia?"

"Whether I find Peri or not, I'll be going back to Tucson and pick up where I left off."

"If that's your plan either way, why all the effort to find her?"

"The best answer to that is, why not? I'd like to find her and see how she's doing and what she's been up to. If I thought it might go further than that, I'd jump at the chance. I just don't think it will."

"You're doing a hell of a lot of traveling, just to see how she's doing. You could probably find the answer to that with a phone call."

"Maybe. I'd like to see her too, no matter what. At the least, she's been a good friend over the years, and seeing old friends is always better than just a phone conversation."

"It is that. Other than visit some relatives while you're here are you going to do anything else?"

"I hadn't planned anything, other than maybe stopping by and having a couple of beers with you."

"Are you going to take a look at your farm and see what they're doing with it?"

"I doubt it. There will be too much wreckage and ruin for me to look at. It would hurt, I think, after all the effort Mary and I put into building up the land. Not to mention the way we left the wild parts wild. I know that's all changed now. All I'll find there now is roads and houses. The farm is gone."

"If I were you, Ken, I'd feel the same way. It's funny isn't it, the way everything changes when you start to get old, yet so much stays the same."

"Yeah, the good passes us by. Your folks are gone, my folks are gone, Nancy and Mary are gone, but all the crap that's been there all of our lives is still around."

"I guess we can't complain too much though. For a couple of old men like us, life could be a whole lot worse."

"It could. I don't feel that old anyway, so much as I miss those things I had when I was young. Maybe that's why I'm trying so hard to find Peri. Maybe if I find her, part of being young will return. At least for a little while."

"If she can do that for you, I hope for your sake, you do find her. If it would do the same for me, I'd be going to Georgia with you, no matter how much I hate traveling."

"Even if it's only for a few moments, having some of those feelings I had back then would be great. I don't know if it would make getting old easier or harder, but either way, they would be worth it."

"If you could live it all over again, Ken, would you?"

"You're damn right I would. Whether it was exactly the same or everything changed, I'd do it again. My only hope would be that I could do it better next time."

"I would too. I'd sure like to crawl in bed with Nancy again, the way it was a few years ago."

"I feel the same way. I'd like to do it all. The farm, the wading around some construction site with the mud over my ankles, all of it."

"And Peri?"

"And Peri. My life with Mary was better than anything I ever deserved, but Peri was part of my life too. I don't think I'd want to change that."

"What would Mary have said if she knew how you felt about Peri all those years?"

"That she understood."

"Really?"

"Yes, really. She knew about Peri. She knew about her the whole time."

Bill didn't have any more questions, so we were quiet for a while. We were both tired too, so we didn't talk much the rest of the way. When he dropped me off, I told him I'd see him again before I left for Georgia.

I was sure he didn't understand how Mary could have known how I felt about Peri and not be upset by it. I wasn't sure myself. The only thing that made sense was the fact that Mary didn't feel threatened by it. She wasn't because we had a great relationship and because she always knew I loved her. Part of our good relationship also came, I believe, because we worked so well together. It didn't matter what needed doing, we always managed to get it done as a team. It was especially true with the farm, even if she always did more of the work than I did.

The jobs she didn't want to do were all connected to the tractor. Early our first spring, we purchased an old Farmall M. Mary tried driving it, and even though she could handle it, she was extremely nervous, so from then on, at her request, I did all the tractor work.

The first year, the plowing was rough going. None of the ground was plowed since the thirties, so the sod was heavy, and because the soil was sand, the gopher runs were numerous. In spots, there were so many running together that the rear wheel would drop down deep enough to hang up the tractor. Every time it happened, I had to dig it out with a shovel. It was slow going.

I only plowed a little over an acre and had to go over the ground a half-dozen times with the disc to smooth out the ground enough to make it possible to work. Even then, we were left with occasional clods of sod to deal with.

"It'll be better next year," I told Mary as we worked our way around the rough spots.

"It's better than I expected, Ken. This land hasn't had anything planted in it for a long time."

She was satisfied with my soil preparations. The tomatoes and peppers she started in the basement with grow lights were a different story. The quality of the plants was good. The problem was that there weren't near as many as it seemed there were before we planted them. We filled the empty ground with a lot of summer squash, radish, sweet corn, green beans, and melons.

I knew she would always be disappointed with the number of plants she could start that way, so I built her a greenhouse during the summer. I dug the footings with a posthole digger. I built walls three feet high and sheeted them with plywood. The roof was framed with two by fours. I covered it and the end walls with Plexiglas and caulked the seams between the four by eight sheets with silicon. One of the heating guys I knew installed a used LP gas furnace for me, and I did the wiring myself. It was minimal, so it was easy, and perfection wasn't required.

Every year, I plowed up more ground until the tilled land amounted to about twelve acres. We never planted any more than two-thirds of the land in vegetables. The other third I planted to rye in the fall and buckwheat in the late spring, both of which I plowed down to add humus to the soil.

We mulched all the rows with oat straw every year, and Mary cultivated between the rows with a rear-mounted rototiller.

Mary was strictly organic, so everything we put back in the ground was a big asset. She never used chemical fertilizers or pesticides, yet the soil constantly improved and the crops were increasingly better every year.

She planted all the peppers in wide rows, so the yield for the amount of space they took up was very high.

She did the same with onions, radishes, spinach, carrots, and lettuce, but they were secondary crops, so the yield wasn't as important. She always did well with summer squash too. It was the peppers and tomatoes though, where the real profit was.

During the spring planting, we were both out in the fields on weekends. All the peppers and tomatoes went in by hand. We quickly developed a good system. We marked the rows first, and then I went ahead and dug the holes with a hoe, which I could do by eye.

Mary followed behind with a hose hooked up to the irrigation system she designed and I put together. She filled the holes with water, and before she was done, I was setting out the plants. I carried a flat of them and dropped a plant in each hole. When Mary finished with the water, she followed behind me, down on her hands and knees, putting each plant into the ground. When the plants were laid out, I followed behind her, on my hands and knees putting plants in the ground. The last thing we did each day was a second watering.

With the exception of potatoes, Mary planted all the crops from seed herself. The early crops like radishes, lettuce, carrots, and onions went in before the plants, and the rest didn't get planted until after school was out, so she managed to get it all done without any difficulty.

Mary loved flowers, so every year after the field crops were planted, she filled several flowerbeds in the front yard with annuals she started in the greenhouse. By midsummer, the yard was always an ocean of color.

Mary did almost all of the harvesting herself, even later in the summer when the crops were coming in the heaviest. By then, it was an everyday job.

During marketing time, it took both of us to finish up the washing, sorting, and packing of the vegetables Friday evening. It wasn't unusual for it to be close to midnight by the time we finished loading the one-ton stake truck we used to haul everything to market.

After the truck was loaded, no matter what time it was, Mary always said, "It's going to be a good day at the market tomorrow."

Unless I had to work on Saturday, which was rare, I went with Mary to the market. When the produce was heaviest, I stayed until we finished. Early and late summer, when the produce was lighter, I followed her there, helped her set up the tables, and then went back home. She was fast and great with customers, so she had no trouble handling it alone.

While the kid was still too young to stay home alone, he came along. He spent the time at market in the cab of the truck, sleeping.

While we were setting up, starting before five in the morning, Mary always put the display together. She always knew how she wanted it. She also knew what she'd charge for each item and made signs for them. That way, a customer never needed to ask how much for something.

We also displayed a large sign saying all our vegetables were organically grown. Because our prices were competitive and the vegetables were organic, sales were always good.

I packaged the vegetables in various size trays and then continued to package and keep the tables full as the day wore on. Mary took care of most of the customers, but when it got real busy, I waited on them too.

At the end of the day, Mary gave away all the produce we weren't going to can or freeze to people she knew that really needed it, and if there was a lot, she gave it to a church group that delivered it to the local meals-on-wheels group.

It was always an extremely tiring day, even if we sold out early, but Mary loved every minute of it. She loved dealing with the people there, whether it was other growers or customers, many of whom she knew by name. I liked the work, sounds, and smells of the market. I was never anywhere near as good with people as she was though.

The best thing about it was the joy Mary got out of it. She enjoyed the market as much as she did farming, and that was what mattered to me the most.

It became a tradition on market day after the truck was unloaded and the market materials and boxes and crates used to haul the produce in were stashed away in Mary's garden shed for her to thank me for helping and give me a hug and kiss.

I always kissed her back and then touched in one intimate spot or another. Laughing, she pushed me away, saying, "Not until tonight, you dirty old man," knowing all the time we were too tired for anything anyway.

Even so, on the rare occasions we managed an afternoon nap, it was always very pleasant feel her warm body lying next to mine.

CHAPTER 9

I thought about visiting various relatives and quickly realized I wasn't really in the mood. Even though I had a lot of cousins I liked and enjoyed, I didn't feel like explaining why I made the trip. I knew I could easily lie about the reasons I did. I wasn't in the mood for that either. The same was true of friends. So the only visit I made was to my favorite aunt and uncle.

When they asked me why I was in Minnesota, I told them the main reason was to visit them. They laughed, knowing I wasn't being totally honest. They let it go at that anyway.

We had a nice visit in the morning, they took me out to lunch, and then I left. I stopped by Bill's. He wasn't home. I thought about waiting around, then decided I'd see him the next day when he was expecting me.

With nothing else to do, I went to the Sherburne National Wildlife Refuge, which is north and west of Zimmerman, Minnesota. I hiked the Blue Hill Trail about five miles. It turned into another reminder of the past and the life I once had with Mary.

We hiked all the trails in the refuge together often, except the busy times of spring and summer. Most of the hikes were in the fall during the change of seasons and occasionally in the winter during the years the snow wasn't too heavy.

I took a lot of pictures on the hike, and when I finished, I drove the wildlife drive and took a lot more. It was a reasonably pleasant afternoon. There was still a fair amount of day left when I finished, so I did what I wasn't going to do and shouldn't have done. I drove by our farm.

It was a sad thing to see. All of it was divided into lots and filled with paved roads. Even from the main road, I could see that the big stand of pines Mary and I spent some time under all those years ago were gone, cut down to put a road exactly where some twit wanted it.

Close to a dozen houses were already built, and three more were under construction. I hated the sight of them and couldn't help but wonder what it was I thought I was doing all the years I was part of the same kind of thing. And I thought Peri put me on a few guilt trips. They were nothing compared to this.

On the way to the RV park, I stopped at a bar in Princeton and drank a couple of stiff Jack Daniels and water. I would have had a few more, only I knew better than to do it when I still had to drive.

I told Bill about it when I visited him the next day.

"So it bothers you now, Ken, about being a carpenter, after you saw what they did to your farm?"

"It bothers me. I feel like I could have done more to help the environment instead of doing so much to destroy it."

"We all could have done more. We could all do more now. Everyone shares the guilt. The thing is, you did more than most of us. Think about how you and Mary farmed all those years. Constantly improving the soil instead of killing it with chemicals."

"That was mostly Mary. All I did was help her."

"No, you did more than just help. It's true that Mary did most of the farming. You both agreed about how you would farm though, and I know you were the one who insisted that you leave most of the farm the way you found it. You could have made some money if you cut down the full-grown oaks and maples out in your woods and sold them to a mill."

"It's all gone now, Bill."

"Maybe so. It would have been gone many years ago if someone else owned it. As far as you being a carpenter, you were simply trying to make a living, the same as the rest of us."

"Maybe. I still think I should have found a better way."

"What the hell is better? Working for some giant corporation that doesn't give one damn about anything other than the bottom line. Money only is all they care about. The hell with anything and everything else, no matter what it is. They own the media and the minds of most people. The problem is bad education, advertising, ignorance, and a news media that sucks shit."

"Yeah, I know. Ignorance is bliss when you're stupid. Religion surely doesn't help any either."

"It never has, Ken. The only reason it was created was so the powers that existed at the time it was invented could use it to control people's minds. Nothing's changed. They're still doing it."

"I know. Sometimes I think I'm lucky to be as old as I am. I've already had a damn good life. Think of what the kids today are going to go through when it all comes crashing down. The environmental problems alone will eventually kill billions of us."

"If it doesn't drive us to extinction. You're right about us being lucky. Day to day, this getting old seems hard. Yet when you think about it, you and I don't have anything to complain about. It hurts a lot when we lose someone, the way we both did with our wives. But we still have to remember how lucky we were to have had them for so long in the first place."

"True. It'd still be nice, Bill, to be able to find a way to solve some of the problems."

"It would. The thing is, we both do what we can. Neither you nor I have the money, power, or influence to solve the problems that have grown to such huge proportions. All we can do is stay informed and not believe or follow the rich and powerful and their nasty conservative ways. We make every attempt to vote right. And in our day-to-day living, we try to screw up as little of the planet as we can. If everyone did that, the world would be a different place."

"That's true. We'll have to do something about education for anything to change, and I think it's highly unlikely we will."

"Ken, it's highly unlikely any of the things we'd like to see change ever will. Which is why what you said about us being lucky to be the age we are is true. I wouldn't want to grow up in the environment the kids of today are in."

"Me either. Not the human or the real part of it."

"By the real part, I assume you mean the wild places."

"What few of them are left. No matter where you go now, you'll find people or signs they were there. And the signs are never good."

"You're right about that, Ken. There's very little left, and it won't be long before it's all gone. If it were up to the Republicans, all the national parks and wildlife refuges would be eliminated. Just think of the theme park Disney could build in Yellowstone."

"And the oil drilling, timbering, and mining the corporate world could accomplish. Not to mention the wondrous vacation homes to be built for the rich and famous in all of those for now beautiful places."

"Depressing, isn't it?"

"It can be if you let it, Bill. Like you said though, I just try to do what I can, and I also try to enjoy what's left, even if it isn't as pristine as it ought to be. Living in Tucson, it's easy to get away from the day to day. The farthest I ever have to drive is when I hike Madera Canyon in the Santa Rita Mountains, and they're only fifty miles away. Most of my hikes are less than a ten-mile drive."

"You're lucky to have that. It's a long drive to any place wild from here in South Minneapolis."

"I know, Bill. I'm definitely going to Georgia, but I'm already starting to miss Arizona."

"So when are you leaving for Georgia?"

"In the wee small hours tomorrow morning, probably about two or three."

"Why so damn early?"

"It's a good time to drive. Other than trucks, there's not much traffic. I also like to drive a lot of miles every day, and I hate driving during the evening hours. So I leave early and quit earlier than I otherwise would."

"Do you get enough sleep that way?"

"I always do."

And I did. I went to bed shortly after seven that night and was up and on the way shortly after two. I wasn't at all tired. All I felt was anxious, partly to see Marge and Walt again, but mostly to see Peri. If she was actually in Georgia when I got there.

I took Highway 10 out of Elk River to I694. I94 followed, and it took me into Wisconsin. It's a pretty drive along that stretch of freeway. I just didn't see any of it in the dark.

It was all freeways until I reached Georgia. After I94, I picked up I90 to Rockford, Illinois. From there, it was I39 through flat Illinois countryside, with nothing to see but cornfields, which had stopped growing and were turning brown.

Next was I74 to I57, which took me into Southern Illinois. There weren't a lot of rest stops on any of the freeways, and it was late in the evening when I finally found one and parked. I knew I could stay there for several hours without upsetting anyone, so after I used the restroom, I crawled into bed. I slept well for about five hours and was on the road again.

The farther south I drove, the heavier the traffic became. I picked up I24 while I was still in Illinois, and even with the traffic, I made decent time until I reached Nashville, where there was some kind of backup that took two hours to get through.

At Chattanooga, I switched to I75, which took me into Georgia. From there, it was a short drive before I left the freeway for Georgia back roads.

What little of the scenery I could see in Tennessee and Kentucky, given the traffic, it was pretty. Off the freeway and on the back roads, Georgia was beautiful. I drove over a hundred miles of them on the way to Marge's, and it was a pleasant ride all the way.

Almost all the roads and highways were two lanes, winding through the North Georgia Mountains. It was the first time I'd seen most of it, so I slowed down and enjoyed the ride.

Marge lived in subdivision off Highway 136, not far from Highway 60. There was a small RV park about four miles west of there and they had an open spot.

As soon as I settled in, I called Marge on her cell phone. I thought she would still be working for another couple of hours and planned to leave her a message telling her where I was. Instead, she answered the phone.

"This is your brother," I told her, "and I'd like to come and visit."

"Oh, really. When?"

"As soon as it's convenient for you. Say, in an hour or two."

"What do you mean, an hour or two? Where the hell are you?"

"In an RV park, about four miles from your house."

"I wish you would have called before you came, Ken. This is not a good time."

"Why not? What's wrong?"

"There's nothing wrong. Peri is here. She flew in today. That's why I'm home. I picked her up at the airport. I hate to tell you this, but Peri has some problems and I don't think she wants to see anyone right now."

"I know something's going on with Peri," I told Marge and then told her about my quest to find Peri and how it started, emphasizing the fact that Peri had stopped by the house in Tucson. "So ask Peri if it will bother her to see me. If she says it will, fair enough. I'll head back to Tucson tomorrow morning. Call me when you know."

I gave her my cell phone number and hung up.

I expected a long wait. A long ten minutes later, Marge called. "Peri's laughing so hard she can't talk right now. She says, however, that it will be wonderful to see you. Especially since you are obviously still you. So come over anytime. We are all going out to dinner tonight."

I took a shower in the RV, put on a fresh change of clothes, and went to Marge's.

CHAPTER 10

Walt was home from work when I got to Marge's. He gave me a hug the way he always did when we hadn't seen each other for a while. Marge did the same, and then last, I got the hug I wanted most, from Peri.

I put my hands on her shoulders. Smiling, I looked at her as I held her away from me.

"You are still one very beautiful lady," I said. "It sure is good to see you again."

She smiled back at me, even though there were tears in her eyes. "It's good to see you too," she said softly and gave me another hug. Then she kissed me, putting more into it than a simply "I'm glad to see you" feeling. We hugged again and held on for a few moments.

Walt and Marge pretended they didn't notice.

"We are having a glass of wine," Marge said finally. "Would you like one?"

"A beer would be better," I answered.

"That figures. You really *are* still you."

I followed Marge into the kitchen when she went to get me the beer.

"Someday," she said as she handed me the beer, "you will have to tell me about you and Peri. Between you two, there is sure a hell of a lot more than just friendship."

She smiled, and we left the kitchen.

While they finished their wine and I finished my beer, the conversation was kept to small talk about times past, families, and old friends.

We went out to eat at a Mexican restaurant in Murrysville, a small town less than three miles from their house. I'd never been there before because we rarely ate out when Mary and I were there. It was too difficult for Mary to control her diet when we did.

Walt drove, and as soon as Peri and I got in the back seat, she took my hand and squeezed it lightly. It sent shivers up my spine. I for sure knew then that my odyssey to find her hadn't been wasted.

The time I would have with her now was going to be worth the effort I made to find her, no matter how short it was or what we did with it. My mission was finding Peri Gray, and for however short a time, I had found her.

The restaurant was a cute little place, run by a young and very friendly Mexican man. He was full of smiles when he saw Walt and Marge.

"How are you, Walt, and you, Marge," he said when we went inside and he showed us to a booth.

"We're good." Marge said. "This our friend, Peri, and my brother Ken. They're here in Georgia for a visit."

"It's always nice to meet friends and relatives of Walt and Marge," he said to Peri and me, smiling widely. "I hope you enjoy your meal."

He brought us the menus and, then without asking, brought a pitcher of beer, Walt's favorite brand. The place didn't serve any other alcoholic beverages. Walt poured three glasses. Peri drank water.

We talked about the food while we decided what to eat. It wasn't until after we ordered that the conversation became more serious. What I wanted to talk about was why Peri was traveling all over the country. The last thing I wanted to do at that point though, was to upset her, so I didn't ask.

Walt is the one who got the conversation moving in the right direction.

"I don't know what you're doing here exactly, Ken," he said. "From the little I've been told, you went to Minnesota and then came here based on a phone call you got in Arizona."

"That's where it started. After the call, I missed Peri by no more than two minutes. I didn't have any idea what was going on, so I decided to go to Minnesota to ask her."

"What I want to know," Peri asked, "is how you knew I was coming here? Only a couple of people knew. Bill wasn't one of them."

"Will you get mad at anyone if I tell you?"

"No. I'm just curious."

"My first day in Minnesota, I went up to Sturgeon Lake with Bill. Jen told me you were coming here. She wouldn't tell me why nor would she tell me why you've been traveling all over the country."

"And you'd like to know."

"Only if you want to tell me. For me, the most important thing is that you're here and I've found you here. The rest would be nice to know. It's just not as important as this."

Peri hesitated a moment, sighed, and said, "I guess I might as well tell you and get it over with."

"Only if you want to," I said.

"I want to. I owe you that much, Ken."

Her story scared me and filled me with dread. She had cancer again, and it had spread a lot. She went through chemotherapy and radiation when she had breast cancer and again when the cancer returned. Her doctor in Minnesota told her that if they treated her with it a third time, it could kill her. Even the Mayo Clinic told her there wasn't anything they could do for her. So she was looking into alternative treatments. She also said that Bill didn't know about the cancer reoccurring or her second round of chemo and radiation because it happened right after Nancy died. She didn't want to put any more burdens on him then and decided not to do it until it was absolutely necessary.

"This is the last clinic I'm checking out," she said. "All of them want me to spend at least a month with them as an outpatient to start with. I haven't decided which one I'll be going to yet. It obviously won't be until I finish here. The two I like best so far are one in Minnesota and the one in Tucson."

"Peri," I said, "if you decide the clinic in Tucson is the one you're going to, I have a big house with a spare bedroom. You're more than welcome to stay with me. You can come and go however you want and need to, and it won't be any kind of a problem. It'll be a lot cheaper than paying for a motel and eating out all the time."

"Thank you for the offer, Ken. I'll let you know. It is expensive to do what I've been doing. That's why I called Marge to see if it would be okay to stay with her and Walt. If I decide on Tucson, and that's a very big if, I might take you up on your offer."

Given our past, I was sure Tucson wouldn't be the clinic she chose no matter how much I wanted it to be, but at least, she left me some hope.

Peri ordered the shrimp fajitas, and I noticed that she purposely didn't eat the tortillas or any of the toppings on the lettuce or tomatoes that came with her meal. In the past, I'd never seen her be so careful about what she ate. I wondered if her cancer had something to do with it.

"How has your trip been so far?" Walt asked. "Have you put a lot of miles on the RV?"

"The trip's been good, if a bit tiring. The best thing is, I had a goal when I started and I've made it. I've driven the RV over three thousand miles, and the car around a hundred. There'll be another eighteen hundred miles on the RV when I get back to Tucson."

"That's a lot of driving," Marge said.

"It is, and speaking of driving, you said you picked up Peri at the airport. I thought you always rode Marta there?"

"I did both. I drove to the North Springs Station, rode Marta to the airport, and met Peri. I didn't want her to ride Marta alone the first time."

"I think it's a good way to do it," Peri said. "It was much simpler than the usual parking hassles you have at airports."

"It is, in an airport as big as Atlanta's," I agreed. "In Tucson, we don't need anything like Marta because it's a much smaller city with a smaller airport than Atlanta."

"Tucson," Walt said, "is the easiest airport to deal with I've ever seen."

Our conversation continued with more small, irrelevant topics throughout the meal. It seemed as though all of us, Peri included, were avoiding the reason both of us were visiting Georgia.

We were near the end of the meal when Walt asked, "So how is everyone in Minnesota?"

"I didn't do much visiting," I told him. "The few people I saw were fine."

I gave them a brief rundown of whom I saw and how I spent my time.

"So you spent more time with Bill than anyone."

"I did. I'm always happy to see him. We always have a lot to talk about, especially politics, the environment, and such. Our conversations are always lively, yet we almost never disagree. He's been an incredibly good friend for all the years I've known him. I could never have a better one."

"What about me?" Peri asked.

I didn't answer her. I couldn't answer her. I just smiled. She returned it, giggled, and then we both laughed. Walt and Marge gave us curious looks. Peri blushed when she noticed their expressions.

"It's been known," I said, "for our relationship to go beyond simple friendship. Especially when we were young."

When Walt and Marge smiled at my comment, they tried not to let them show too much. Peri gave me the evil eye even though she couldn't hide her smile either. Then we suffered a short, somewhat uncomfortable silence.

"What are your plans now, Ken," Walt asked finally, "since you've found Peri and got the answers you were looking for? Are you going back to Tucson?"

"I'm going back to Tucson," I said, pausing to see Peri's reaction. It was what I hoped for. "Not right now though. I want to spend some time with you and Marge, along with Peri, now that I'm here. Even if I hadn't been this lucky and found her I'd stay for a while. Going back right away without visiting some would be very stupid after driving all those miles."

"Good. I thought you might go back with Marge and me both working and Peri busy during the day too."

"I can stay busy during the day. I've got my cameras along, and there are a lot of interesting places around here I haven't seen yet."

"Other than working," Marge said, "the only time we'll be busy is Friday night. We have a meeting at church. So don't go to Helen or Dahlonega when you're out exploring. Walt and I will take you there this weekend. I think Peri will get a kick out of them, and it'll give us something to do."

Marge was never much interested in going places requiring a lot of exercise. Visiting parks and waterfalls did, so it wasn't a surprise that she wanted to take to towns for something to do.

"You've got a deal. As for Friday, I'll take Peri out to dinner. I promise to bring her home early and safe."

Peri shook her head slightly at my comment.

"Now," Marge said, "I think it's time to go home. It's been a long day for all of us and Peri will be very busy tomorrow. Not to mention that Walt and I have to work."

"I agree," I said, even though I would have liked to spend more time with Peri. "It has been a long day."

I didn't go in when we got back to their house.

"Is it okay," I just asked, "if I stop over tomorrow night?"

"It's up to Peri," Marge said.

"I'd like that," Peri said.

I was a happy person when I went back to the RV park. I quickly realized, too, that Marge was right about ending the evening early. I was suddenly very tired and the bed looked inviting. I crawled in and quickly fell asleep. I slept sound and didn't wake up until shortly before sunrise.

CHAPTER 11

I walked around the RV park a couple of times as I watched
the sunrise. It wasn't much of a walk and thought about going
out on Price Road (Highway 136) for a longer one. I decided
not to, knowing I'd walk a fair amount when I got to one of the
parks.

I looked at the map and decided to go to Amicalola Falls
State Park first. The falls there were the highest waterfalls east of
the Mississippi in the United States, so it seemed like a good place
to start.

Since I was hungry, on the way there, I stopped at the Waffle
House at the intersection of Highways 60 and 400. Waffle Houses
have great hash browns, so I ate a double order, smother and covered,
which meant they came with cheese and onions. I also had three
eggs, over medium, sausage, bacon, and wheat toast. Not the most
nutritious meal one could eat. It was delicious nonetheless.

I stopped at the visitor center at the park and bought a book on
North Georgia hiking trails, in case I decided to explore more than
the usual tourist attractions.

Just before the half-mile walk to the falls, there's a small pool.
Several people were sitting around it fishing. It reminded me of a
place in Arizona, up in the Catalina Mountains, called Rose Canyon
Lake. It's only a man-made puddle of water, but anything more than
three gallons is a lake there.

I hiked around it once, and the people fishing were getting excited about catching fish not much more than three inches long. What was happening at the pool here in Georgia appeared to be about the same.

After spending most of my life in Minnesota, the land of way more than ten thousand real lakes, and having done a lot of fishing, I couldn't imagine how anyone could get excited about catching the kind and size of fish they were.

I never caught a fish larger than ten pounds in all my years in Minnesota, although I fished with a lot of people who did better. I have vivid memories of watching my father the time he hooked a twenty-pound northern pike on light tackle. I was about sixteen, and we were on vacation in Northern Minnesota, fishing Cass Lake, near the town of Bemidji.

Dad had to fight it for over an hour before the fish was tired enough to be reeled in. When I finally got the net under it and it was in the boat, we discovered that it was barely hooked in the mouth.

"That's a fantastic fish, Dad," I told him. "I'll bet he'll be some good eating too."

"I don't think so," Dad said. "Get him unhooked. He's not seriously injured, so I'm throwing him back."

"Why?"

"Because he gave me one hell of a fight and he deserves to live another day. Besides, fish his size are good for the lake."

I wonder now what people who catch and keep fish three inches long would say about doing something like that. At the time, I was disappointed when Dad threw him back. Now I admire him for it. It was the right thing to do and taught me a lot about what's really important in life.

I took a lot of pictures as I walked back to the falls, and even more as it came into view. It was an impressive sight. Close to the falls there were steps to climb to the base and a lot more to the top of the falls. Six hundred in all.

As impressive as the falls were, they were a bit of a letdown. There were too many people; the paths, stairs, and viewing platforms were too manicured. It would be a lot nicer if it were more rustic and natural.

I walked back down some trails rather than the stairs. Even they were way too people oriented and not near natural enough. Still, I knew that having a park there at all was better than what a lot of people would have done with the place.

And even though I was a bit disappointed with the park, I knew that if I hiked even part of the eight-mile trail that started in the park, which went to the beginning of the Appalachian Trail, I would find it different, more natural, and wilder.

I probably would have hiked some of it if I weren't already so tired from all the traveling. Instead I left the park and went back to the RV and took a nap. I felt a lot better when I got to Marge and Walt's.

They took Peri and me out to a Chinese buffet. It was in a shopping center on Highways 400 and 53. The food was decent, and it gave Peri the chance to pick out what she wanted since she was being so careful about what she ate.

It was one of the few places Mary and I went on previous visits, so it was familiar to me. As I have a tendency to do at buffets, I ate way too much and thoroughly enjoyed it. Peri seemed to enjoy it too, even if most of her food did come from the salad bar.

We called it a night again after we ate and went right back to the house. The last thing Peri said before I left was, "You're taking me out tomorrow night then."

"Is tomorrow Friday?" I asked.

"Yes, it is. You didn't know that?"

"I've been traveling so much, I had no idea what day it was. I will for sure be here to take you out tomorrow night anyway. Even if I didn't know what day it is."

"Good," she said, then kissed me goodbye. It was a good thing she wasn't my sister, or all of us would have had some strange thoughts.

Peri was on my mind until I fell asleep. When I did, I was tired enough to sleep sound and dream very little. I woke up early, as usual, and went out to explore more of Georgia without eating breakfast right away.

I decided to have a breakfast sandwich on the run this time rather than stop somewhere. I drove into Gainesville and picked up a couple of chicken, egg, and cheese biscuits at Chick-fil-A. It was a few miles out of the way. That didn't bother me, their biscuit sandwiches are worth it, especially their biscuits.

I took Highway 129 out of Gainesville to Cleveland and then Highway 75 to Helen. Just east of Helen is Unicoi State Park, and next to the park is Anna Ruby Falls. I stopped there first.

The falls were about a half-mile from the parking lot. It was a nice walk, even if it did suffer from the same overdone amenities as Amicalola Park. It was also too crowded with people. I still managed to take a lot of pictures on the way and at the falls.

Anna Ruby Falls are special because there are actually two falls next to each other. Two creeks run together where the falls start, and it is an impressive sight. They weren't as big or high as Amicalola, but in their own way, they were even more beautiful.

After the falls, I drove around Unicoi State Park. It's a nice, well-kept place, which didn't have anything of particular interest to me.

I still had most of the day left so I headed north on 75, rather than go back to the RV. Waiting there until it was time to pick up Peri would have made for a very long day.

I drove to Hiawassee, an interesting town next to Chatuge Lake, another man-made body of water, which was a large one this time.

I wasn't particularly hungry yet. I stopped at Hardee's for a hamburger and fries anyway, just because I kind of like their burgers.

From Hiawassee, I drove west on 75 to Blairsville. I didn't stop until I saw a small meat market as I was leaving. I stopped there and bought some home-smoked bacon and homemade sausage, knowing either one would be good for breakfast or any other meal. I was also about out of meat in the RV.

From Blairsville, it was 129 south, another beautiful drive on two-lane, winding mountain roads. I drove past Blood Mountain and then stopped at Desoto Falls. I took the long walk back to the high falls first and, of course, took a lot of pictures. The walk to the lower falls is a more difficult than the other path. It's a fair amount shorter, but a lot steeper than the path to the upper falls. Both of the falls were interesting, although not near as impressive as either Amicalola or Anna Ruby.

When I got back to the RV, I showered, shaved, and put on a clean change of clothes and still had an hour to wait before it was time to pick up Peri. It was one of the longest hours I've ever spent. I was anxious to see her yet nervous about how it would go with just the two of us. Years had gone by since we'd been alone together.

Walt, Marge, and Peri were each having a glass of red wine when I got there. Marge brought me a beer without asking me what I wanted.

"Where are you going to eat tonight?" Marge asked as I opened my beer.

"I thought we might try that steak house out on 400. If it's okay with Peri."

"Any place is fine," Peri said. "Even if I can't eat steak, I'm sure they'll have some kind of salad."

"Why don't you take her to Ryan's?" Walt suggested. "It's a buffet, and the food is decent. That way, Peri can pick out what she wants."

"That sounds better," Peri said. "It'll be a lot easier for me. I'm not in the mood for anything fancy."

"Okay," I agreed. "Ryan's it is."

I was hoping to eat someplace more intimate and quiet, where we could carry on a decent conversation. I just wasn't about to suggest anything that wouldn't be the best for Peri.

We left when I finished my beer. Peri still had wine in her glass she obviously didn't want. It was a quiet ride to the restaurant. Neither one of us had much to say until we went through the buffet and sat down to eat. I was still so nervous my appetite was about gone, so all I had on my plate was a couple of pieces of fried chicken and a few fries. Peri's plate was filled with salad.

"Is that all you're eating, Ken?" she asked. "You, at an all-you-can-eat buffet, and there's almost nothing on your plate."

"I'm not that hungry."

"And why not?"

I tried to smile. "Because the truth is, I'm too damn nervous."

"What are you so nervous about?"

"Us. Here. Now. The moment."

"Please explain.

"I've been waiting for and hoping for this exact time since shortly after that phone call I got asking for you, not to mention a good part of my life. Now that it's here, I'm afraid I'll do something or say something really stupid to screw it up. I don't want to screw this up, Peri, so I'm nervous."

She reached across the table, laying her hand over mine, squeezing lightly. "It's not going to be like that, Ken. It's not going to be like that at all."

"I wish I could be as sure about it as you are."

"Be sure, Ken, be sure." She gave me her best smile. "You know, when you told Marge you would bring me home safe and early, I damn near choked. Home safe and early? I never."

"I didn't want you to feel uncomfortable about going out with me alone."

"Oh, right! With our history, I'm going to feel uncomfortable going out alone with you. Not hardly."

"I didn't want Marge to worry either."

"Like Marge is going to worry about what you and I do? I think not. Before you got there tonight, I told Marge that it would be a late night tonight, so we would be meeting them at their house in the morning. What do you think she said?"

"I afraid to guess."

"Good plan. Nothing else. Just, good plan. So now will you stop being nervous?"

"I'll do my best."

"You do that, and start by eating something."

I ate a little more, concentrating more on watching her than eating. She was still a very beautiful woman, even with a few lines in her face. They were okay, most of them came from where the smiles had been.

"I've wondered for a long time," I told her, "why the relationship you and I had changed the way it did a few years ago. You've always been as friendly as you ever were, yet there was always something different about it. What happened?"

"It's called breast cancer. I had reconstructive surgery afterward. It helped, it just didn't help enough. I'm not the same woman I was. I was afraid to let you see me."

"What about now?"

"I'm still not totally sure. The difference now is the way you look at me. It's the same look I used to see when we were young. You remember that, don't you, Ken? When we were young?"

"I most surely do. I remember the first time I ever saw you, Peri. It was our second day in the neighborhood. I immediately fell in love with you. I've been in love with you ever since."

"I thought you loved your wife?"

"I did. I loved Mary very much, I still do. That doesn't mean I didn't or couldn't love you. There are a lot of ways to love, even love between a man and a woman. What I feel about you hasn't ever changed. I think mostly, it's just grown."

"I'm still a little afraid you'll find me ugly."

"I don't think that's possible."

"Either way, Ken, let's get out of here, I want to see your RV. We'll see how you feel then."

"It's a bit of a mess. I wasn't expecting any company, so I haven't cleaned since I got here."

"What do you mean, you weren't expecting any company? You traveled the way you did to find me, and you didn't expect me to see your RV if you found me?"

"That's the truth. I didn't expect anything. I just wanted to find you and to see you and to know you were okay. I haven't thought beyond that."

"Sometimes, Ken, you are a little strange. It's a very nice strange, nonetheless, strange it is. Now let's get the hell out of here."

On the ride to the RV, Peri sat as close to me as she could with bucket seats. I showed her around, which didn't take long, given the lack of much space.

"It looks pretty clean to me," she said. "After most men traveled as much as you have lately, this would be a pigsty."

"I like to keep things reasonably neat."

"You do." She took my hands and held them for a few moments, looking into my eyes. "I want you to undress me now. If at any time what you see bothers you, you can take me back to Marge's. I'll understand."

"I like what I see now. It won't change."

"It might. So much of what you and I always were is physical. It could change now. Even without the breast thing, we are both a lot older."

"It's not going to change," I promised. "I've always loved the way you look. I still do."

I didn't stop until I removed all of her clothing.

"Your turn," I said.

I didn't help or hinder her as she undressed me. My jockey shorts were the last to go.

She looked at me, touched me, and smiled. "I see I was wrong to worry. Let's get into bed, Ken. It has been a long time."

It *was* a long time since we'd been there together. It was a long time too, before we left the bed. And that was only for a couple of breaks during the night.

We didn't make love as often as we did in the past. Instead, it was slower, warmer, and meant more than it ever had. She remained as beautiful as ever, the whole time.

My only regret in the morning was knowing we promised to spend the day with Walt and Marge. My fear was that after truly finding Peri Gray again, I would probably soon lose her as I always had in the past.

I watched her as we dressed and couldn't get over how beautiful she was. Before she got too far, I took her in my arms.

"Nothing that has ever happened to you," I said, "has made you any less beautiful than you've always been to me. No matter what happens now, I don't want you to ever forget that."

"Damn it, Ken," she said with a grin, "you shouldn't say things like that when we don't have any time. You are going to pay for it tonight."

"Are you staying with me tonight?"

"Where did you think I was going to stay?"

"At Marge's."

"Don't be silly. I'm staying here tonight and Sunday night. You're giving me a ride to Marta early Monday morning."

"Does Marge know that?"

"Of course. I was supposed to fly out of here this morning. I changed it to Monday when you called Marge, before you got here."

"I'm surprised. Did you do that for me?"

"Sure, I did it for you. I did it for me too. How could I not spend time with a lunatic who drives all over the country looking for me? And I wanted to see you too. More than you'll ever know."

"I'm really glad to hear you say that, Peri. Because nothing I can say to you, or do with you, will ever tell you how happy I am to be with you right now."

CHAPTER 12

When we got to Marge and Walt's in the morning, I finally remembered to give them the presents I bought from Jen's boys for them. They both liked what I gave them, but Marge was particularly impressed.

"Where did you find this?" she asked. "It's hand carved, isn't it?"

"It is. While I was in Minnesota, I met this old guy who lives in the backwoods and does a lot of this kind of work. His name is Kyle Olson, and he's been doing it for years."

"Really, how did you find him?"

Peri's laugh gave me away before I could answer.

"Why are you laughing, Peri?" Marge asked. "Is there something I should know Ken isn't telling me?"

"No," Peri answered, "nothing you should know. Other than your brother is full of it sometimes."

"Oh, it's something imported then."

"Not hardly," I told her. "Kyle is Jen's son. He's all of seventeen. I was just giving you the business because his work has such high quality. Some old guy who's been doing it for years could very well have done it. Jen's youngest son, Lee, made the black walnut pen and letter opener I gave Walt. Pretty incredible, isn't it?"

"I should say so. They are a couple of very talented kids."

"Yes, they are," I agreed, then asked, "So where are you and Walt taking us today?"

"As tired as you two look," Marge said with a grin, "I don't know if we should take you anywhere."

"We are a little tired," I said. "We had a lot of time to make up for last night."

Peri gave me a playful slap on the shoulder.

Marge laughed and Walt rolled his eyes up in his head.

"We decided on Dahlonega," Walt said finally. "We never got around to taking you and Mary there when you were here, and it's a place you and Peri should see. Besides, it's close, so we won't spend much time driving."

"Sounds good," I said, and we went to Dahlonega.

It's a nice little tourist town, filled with small specialty shops, which sell all types of tourist goods. We went through most of them.

Walt and I didn't see a whole lot that interested us initially, but Marge found multitudes of things to show Peri, who was thoroughly enjoying the guided tour.

For me, the first interesting store was selling all manner of Western clothing and leather goods. It was the kind of place one would expect to find in Tucson and often did. The prices were on the high side though, so I didn't buy anything. I did, however, spend a fair amount of money at the fudge shop, where they made all the candy themselves. It turned out to be a foolish thing to do. Peri told me later that she didn't eat anything with sugar. So I gave it all to Marge and Walt.

They wanted to go into the Gold Rush Museum. I refused to go inside. I'd read enough about the things the people in Georgia did to the Cherokee Indians. They forced them all to move to Oklahoma. The trip is called the Trail of Tears. A lot of the Indians died during it.

Knowing what happened was enough to not want anything to do with it. It was supposed to be a big deal because that was where the first gold was discovered in America. To me, it was nothing more than another example of pure greed. I saw no sense in visiting a museum celebrating the worst in mankind.

One of the many jewelry stores had signs in their window, claiming that everything was half price, so we went in. Even though I wasn't much interested, I went in with them anyway.

Marge and Peri were having a good time looking at the earrings when an emerald ring caught my eye. It was one of their more expensive rings, with a large emerald in the center and two smaller ones on each side. All three gems were excellent quality, which were set in a simple gold band.

Emeralds were by far my favorite gemstone, so I told Peri to try it on.

"What for?" she asked.

"Just because I want to see how it looks on you. I love emeralds, and I think they would look good on you."

"I can't afford anything like this."

"I just want to see how it looks."

She tried it on and it fit perfectly. It also looked like it belonged on her. Just as all beautiful things looked as though they belonged on her.

"Do you like it, Peri?"

"That's a dumb question," she said, taking the ring off and handing it to the saleslady. "I love it. It's just too expensive."

I smiled at her.

"Don't even think about it, Ken. There's no way you are buying that for me."

I just shrugged and said, "Okay."

A few doors down from the jewelry store, Peri, Marge, and Walt went into a women's clothing store. I told them I wasn't in the least bit interested in looking at clothes of any kind, let alone women's clothing. As soon as they went inside, I went back to the jewelry store and bought the ring. I knew it was the wrong time to give it to Peri, so I stuffed it in my pocket. All I could do then was hope to be lucky enough to find the right time to give it to her.

We stopped to eat when we left Dahlonega. Since it was on the way back and we all liked the food, we ate Mexican again.

There was still a fair amount of day left afterward, so Marge asked us if we wanted to do anything else. Peri and I were both very tired by then, so we said no. Marge and Walt weren't the least upset about it, and we called it a day.

Before we left them, we decided that since Peri had such an early flight Monday morning, we would keep Sunday short and just have dinner together.

Our talking about Peri leaving got to me. I was already feeling a slight sense of loss even before we got back to the RV.

"You seem kind of down, Ken," Peri said when we got there. "Is something wrong?"

"Nothing's wrong. I was just thinking about you leaving Monday morning and going back to Minnesota. I don't want you to walk out of my life again, the way you always have before."

"You shouldn't even be thinking about that yet. We still have two nights and a full day ahead of us. I think we should try to enjoy the time we have. We can worry about Monday morning on Monday morning."

"I know you're right. It's just that this is different from all the other times we've been together, for however short or long a time. This time, there's no real reason for us not to be together."

"You're forgetting the reason we're both here, aren't you, Ken?"

"No, and I'm not about to. What I'd like to know though, is there really that big a difference between the clinics you've been to? They're all trying to do about the same thing, aren't they?"

"Pretty much, yes. They are all about alternative treatments of cancer. For the most part, the differences are subtle. They are there but minor."

"Is going to the clinic in Tucson out of the question then?"

"Absolutely not."

"Then why not skip the trip back to Minnesota and ride to Tucson with me?"

"Right now, there are too many reasons to even try to talk about. I have to go back Monday, so please try to accept it."

"Okay, I won't bug you about it anymore. I just want you to know that I do care so very much about and for you. It'll be hard when you walk away from me again."

"Just so you know, Ken, I won't be walking away. I'm only going back to Minnesota. Is there some big reason you can't visit me there or I can't see you in Tucson?"

"Of course not."

"Then we shouldn't be having a problem here, should we?"

"We aren't having a problem, Peri. Whatever happens, I'll always want to see you again. It's just that when you're with me and then you're gone again, I'm always scared it'll be the last time."

"I promise that won't happen. We might not have a lot of time, but what time we have, we will share as much as we can."

"I hope so. Haven't you ever regretted, though, the fact that we didn't ever live our lives together? I know I had a damn good life, better than I deserved probably, yet I've always wondered what it would have been if I'd spent it with you."

"There were many times that I wondered the same thing. I always came to the same conclusion after thinking about it. Both you and I were always too impulsive. If we were together when we were young, I doubt it would have worked."

"I still often wish we'd taken the chance."

"I do too, sometimes. The thing is, Mary was much better for you than me. She was steady, she knew what she wanted, and she always kept you on a straight, even path. With her, you always knew who the two of you were and where you were going."

"Why couldn't you and I have had that?"

"I never knew what it was I wanted exactly. I've always looked for something I couldn't find. The worst part is, I was never sure what it was I was looking for. Mary gave you most of what you wanted and what you were looking for. You should be thankful it was her you spent most of your life with and not me."

"Is that why you married Don Gray, because you were looking for something?"

"I think so. When I met him, he seemed so strong, so intelligent, and—"

I couldn't help it. I laughed. It was a harsh, nasty laugh that I immediately regretted.

"What was that about, Ken?"

"I'm sorry, I shouldn't have done that."

"You didn't like Don, did you?"

"No, I didn't. It wasn't because he was with you either. I simply didn't like him. What got to me just now was when you said he was intelligent."

"He was, in a lot of ways."

"He was sometimes a good talker. He could even make some people believe he knew what he was talking about. But intelligent? I don't think so. He was flat-out stupid. I could never respect him, what he said, or what he did."

"Do you think you were smarter than he was?"

"I'm sorry, Peri, I shouldn't have let this conversation get started. He was your husband, and I should know enough to keep my big mouth shut."

"It's too late now, so tell me, do you think you were smarter than he was?"

"Absolutely. I damn sure never would have told you to wear a crystal around your neck and pray harder to get rid of your cancer."

"You believe then, that my cancer now was his fault."

"There's no doubt about it at all."

"And that's why you think he was stupid?"

"That's enough reason. The thing is, everything he believed, preached about, and pretended to know so much about was idiotic."

"Don't you believe in God, Ken?"

"If you mean in the traditional sense, as we were taught in church, no, I don't. Anything spiritual I feel comes from working in a garden or out in the fields. The miracle of putting a tiny seed in the ground and watching it produce food, often enough to feed several people, tells me there's some kind of higher power."

"You mean you think growing food is some kind of miracle?"

"I do. Think about it. When you put a small round radish seed in the ground, in about four weeks, you have something good to eat. Put a lot of them in the ground and you have a lot to eat."

"That's just radishes. A lot of people don't even like them."

"True. A better example is the tomato. You start with an even smaller seed, which grows into a tender little plant. Then put that tender plant in the ground in the harsh, cold land called Minnesota, and before that short growing season you get there is over, you harvest as many as a bushel of tomatoes. What would you call something as awesome as that?"

"I don't know. To me, all it's just something that was always there."

"That's the way most people think about. So they go looking for some mystical bullshit, which has no relevance to anything. Life itself is the real miracle."

"Did you get all those ideas just from raising vegetables?"

"No, I get the same feelings when I'm someplace wild. When I see all the incredible life forms around me, managing on their own without us humans. Life that, in fact, would be better off without us humans, I feel the sense of a higher power. It's long way from the mean-spirited, petty little thing Don Gray called God."

"Wow, I don't remember you having such strong feelings about anything."

"I have them, you and I just never took the time to talk about them. Yours either. Did I upset you, telling you the way I really think about it?"

"No, you haven't. After the life I've lived, I agree with you about a lot of it. The rest, I'm no longer sure."

"That, in my opinion, is a better place to be than where those who are sure tend to be."

Peri smiled then. "You're right you know. You are smarter than Don was."

"And you are beautiful, Peri. Can I take you to bed now, even if it's too early to go to sleep?"

"You better believe it! I can't think of anything I'd rather do right now."

Everything then was soft and warm, slow and easy, and better than anything I expected or thought I deserved. The lingering time after, holding her, was every bit as good.

Later on, we both decided we were hungry. We thought about going out to eat but didn't want to leave the RV. I fried up the bacon I bought at the meat market in Blairsville, a couple of over-easy eggs apiece, and toast.

"Breakfast never tastes this good in the morning," Peri said, even if she didn't eat any of the bacon and ate her toast dry.

"Unless you're like me," I told her, "and wake up hungry most days."

When we fell asleep that night, she had her back against me, and I had my arm around her. Inside, I couldn't shake the fear I was going to lose her again.

We started Sunday slow. Marge and Walt took us out to eat in a small place they liked in Gainesville called the Sunrise Café. The food was good, and they called ahead so the cook had a special salad made ahead of time for Peri.

After we ate, we went to the mall near there and spent some time browsing the bookstore. We visited for a little while when we got back to Marge and Walt's. I told them then I'd be going back to Tucson after I took Peri to the Marta station Monday.

"You haven't been here very long," Marge said.

"I know, and I know I should stay longer. I've been gone for quite a while, so it would be a good idea for me to get home. Next time I come, I'll stay longer."

"I understand," Marge said. "It's been good to have you here, even if it wasn't long."

Peri and I made love again in the late afternoon. After a simple supper in the RV, we went to bed, knowing we had to get up early for Peri's flight. We slept the same way we did Saturday night. I had the same feelings, even stronger this time.

We got up at four Monday morning and left for the Marta station right away. We were real quiet on the ride, with both of us dreading what was coming.

I wanted to ride with her to the airport. She wouldn't let me.

"If you do, it'll be too long of a goodbye. You're going to drop me off in that Kiss Lot Walt and Marge told us about, where you're only allowed to drop me off. Then you're going to let me leave. It's going to hurt enough the way it is."

I kissed her long and hard when I dropped her off and told her I hoped to see her soon.

"It will be as soon as it can be," she said and walked rapidly away from without turning around. Even so, I knew she was crying.

I felt like crying too, but being a typical stupid male, I wouldn't let myself.

I drove straight back to the RV park, hooked up the car to the tow bar, made sure everything was properly stowed away inside the RV, and left for Tucson.

I took Highway 400 to I285, and that to I20, which took me to I10. From there, I was Tucson bound.

There's a lot of pretty countryside to see driving through the south. Alabama is especially beautiful. I saw very little of it. I pushed it hard, stopping only when I needed fuel and when I got too tired to drive. The biggest plus I got from pushing so hard was that I barely noticed West Texas as I drove through it.

My stops to sleep were short. Each time, it was at a rest stop along the freeway, where I slept for a couple of hours, and was on my way again.

I drove into my driveway late Tuesday night, glad to be home, but tired and filled with empty feelings that only come with the sense of having lost. The temperature in Tucson was eighty, yet the house and I were cold.

CHAPTER 13

E ven though I was tired after all the traveling, I was still restless. I spent the first day at home cleaning out the RV, running the dishes through the dishwasher in the house, and all the clothes I took along on the trip through the washer. It used up most of the day.

My restless energy continued, so I spent the evening downloading the pictures I took during the trip. Although I enjoyed looking through the photos, the pictures of Peri that I took in Georgia left me with a hollow sense of loneliness. I found her in Georgia and lost her again, just as I had so many times before. I had the feeling I would never see her again. No matter how close we were, something always happened to keep us apart.

I went to bed late and then woke up early anyway. I got my gear together, put on my boots, and went hiking in the Rincons.

I went on several hikes over the next two weeks. Two long hikes were in Madera Canyon in the Santa Rita Mountains south of Tucson. I hiked Sabino Canyon twice, a couple of trails up on Mount Lemon, and of course, the Rincons.

I was taking a day off from hiking, working on the scrapbook about my traveling when I heard a car door close. It sounded like it was in the driveway. I wasn't expecting any company so I ignored it. Then the doorbell rang and all I could think of was "What are you selling now?"

I was ready to raise hell with whoever it was when I opened the front door. I was shocked, amazed, and so damn happy I nearly wet my pants when a widely smiling Peri stood there on the other side of the door.

"Aren't you going to let me in?" she asked when I just stupidly stood there staring at her.

"Hell, yes," I answered, nearly yelling.

I opened the door wide and finally noticed the two suitcases on the ground on either side of her. She reached down for them. I beat her to the biggest one.

"We'll put these in your room," I said, "and then I'll show you around."

"What makes you think I'm staying, Ken?"

"The suitcases."

We went directly to the guestroom. "Well, this is it, Peri. I hope it'll work okay for you."

She gave me a strange look, walked in the room, and sat down on the bed, facing me. "This is the guestroom you told me about?"

"It is."

She just stared at me for a couple of minutes, then she smiled, shook her head, and started laughing. She laughed so hard tears came to her eyes.

"Ken," she said, "do you really want me to sleep here?"

"Well, it's just, you know," I stammered, "I want you to be comfortable."

"You want me to be comfortable. You don't want to take advantage of me."

"I guess that's about it, yes."

She stood, walked over to me, and put her arms around my neck. I didn't need any more encouragement to kiss her.

"There'll be no guest bedroom for me while I'm here," she said, "so now show me where I'm going to sleep."

I took her into my bedroom.

"This is nice," she said, unbuttoning her blouse. "Now get undressed. We'll discuss everything later. I want this to come first."

I didn't argue. As soon as we were both in bed, she pulled me over her.

"Don't wait for anything," she said.

It happened quickly for both of us, with me going first and her right behind me. I moved my legs outside of hers, pushing hers tight together so she could hold me inside. We lay quietly for a short time before she started moving again, bringing me back. This time it was slow, lasting a long time.

"How long are you going to stay?" I asked after it was over, as we lay close, still holding each other.

"I'm not sure. For the next couple of weeks, I'll be at the clinic every day. They're going to put me on a special diet and teach me how to exercise properly. While that's happening, I'll be getting constant checkups so they're sure that what they're doing is helping."

"Will walking be part of the exercise?"

"Probably."

"Good. I walk every morning and I love to hike. There are a lot of places I'd like to take you if we have more than a couple of weeks."

"It'll be longer. After the first two weeks, they want me to see them twice a week for at least a month. It could be even longer than that."

"I hope it's a lot longer."

It was.

The diet the clinic put her on was more rigid than Mary's was, but not so much that I had any trouble adjusting to it. The biggest differences were the total lack of red meat in it and the carrots. Peri was required to eat at least a half-pound of them every day. She was allowed a minimal amount of seafood or chicken, no more than three times a week, and the rest of the diet was vegetables and fruit, as much raw as possible.

They told her walking was great exercise, and she should walk as much as possible. We started out walking together early every morning, so the first chance we got, I took her to a local sporting goods store for a decent pair of boots.

"These are all too expensive," she complained after trying on a couple of pairs. "I can't really afford anything this fancy."

"It doesn't matter. I can."

"I don't want you to spend your money on me, Ken. My tennis shoes are good enough."

"No, they aren't good enough. So don't argue. I can afford this, and I don't want to take you up in the mountains in any damn tennis shoes. They don't give you near enough support, and they're dangerous where the trails are rough. So pick out a pair and don't argue."

When we left the store, she had her boots, a half-dozen pair of good hiking socks, a CamelBak for water, and a walking stick the right size for her.

Without telling her, I bought her a lightweight DSLR camera with a strong, well-padded strap, so she could take pictures wherever we went. I knew that if we were both taking pictures, it would make a lot better scrapbooking.

We took our first hike after she went to the clinic for a little over a week. I knew she wasn't ready to do any serious climbing, so we hiked the Cactus Forest, which was in Saguaro National Park in the desert just before you start climbing in the Rincons.

We started on the trails at the east end of Broadway, making a circular route. The best trail is the Saguaro Trail. Along a lot of it are ancient saguaro cacti, some of them fifty to sixty feet tall. Peri was surprised at the size of the saguaro and with the amount and variety of life we saw. She loved all of it.

I surprised her with the camera when we were getting ready to start out.

"That looks expensive," she complained. "You shouldn't be spending money on me like this. Besides, I don't know anything about taking pictures."

"It wasn't that expensive, and I'll spend all the money on you I want to. I can afford it. As for not knowing how to take pictures, it doesn't matter. You'll learn."

I explained to her about digital cameras and how she could take as many pictures as she wanted to because they only cost money when you print them. I quickly showed the basics of the camera and told her to take a lot of pictures. She listened, and soon was snapping away at everything, with me her most frequent target.

I took her to Sabino Canyon for our second hike. We rode the tram up to the end and walked down. She loved the canyon, with its high cliffs and rocks on both sides. As soon as we were low enough, we left the road and hiked the rest of the way to the visitor center on the back trails.

Peri said she was impressed with my knowledge of them. I told her that it wasn't anything to be impressed with. I knew them because I'd hiked them so many times.

We took several more hikes over the next two months, gradually going higher in the Rincons, but we hadn't gotten to my favorite hike when she told me she'd finished at the clinic.

"They want me to come for checkups every three months," she explained, "So if you don't mind, I'd like to stay with you when I fly down."

"Of course you can. I have a question though. Why do you have to go back to Minnesota?"

"I'm broke, Ken. I have to go back to work. My boss told me he'd welcome me back when I was ready to work again. I'm ready. I wish I could stay, but I really can't."

"Yes, you can. I have enough money to support both of us. Even if I didn't, I can make decent money as a carpenter here."

"That wouldn't be fair."

"It would be to me, Peri. Money is definitely not an issue, so you have to come up with a lot better argument."

"What will people think if I stay here with you? Aren't you worried about upsetting your family?"

"No, I don't give a damn about what anyone else thinks. Only what you think and want. If what people think is an issue for you, then let's get married."

"Are you serious?"

"Damn right I am. I love you and I want you to live with me. Nothing else matters."

"I can't marry you, Ken. With things the way they are, it would be totally unfair to you."

"I don't think so. Either way, I want you to stay. The only way I'll let you go without any more arguments is if you tell me that you've had enough of me and just don't want to stay."

"That's not it at all. I want to stay, but—"

"The debate is now settled. Married, not married, you *are* staying. The last thing in the world I want now is to lose you again."

"Okay, I'm staying." She smiled. "I was really hoping you wouldn't let me go back. I do love you, and I love it here. I still have to go back though and close up my apartment and decide what to do with the rest of my stuff."

"That's no problem. You ship what you want down here and sell or give away what you don't want. You're going to fly up and back and do everything as fast as you can. I don't want you to be gone any longer than you have to be."

When she flew back to Minnesota I gave her enough money to take care of everything she needed to do. She was only gone a week. For me, it seemed like a month.

The first thing she said when she got back was "God, it's good to be back home. It's so damn cold up there."

I just smiled, and she gave me a big hug and a kiss.

"It's even better to be with you again, Ken. That was the last time I'm ever going to leave you."

She never did.

I waited until after we made love her first night back and then gave her the emerald ring I bought for her in Dahlonega.

"What is this for? When did you buy it?"

"It's for you and because I love you. I bought it the day you tried it on in Dahlonega."

"I can't accept it. It cost way too much. Why did you wait so long to give it to me?"

"You have to accept it. I can't take it back. I waited to give it to you, so that when I did, it wouldn't seem like I was trying to bribe you to come to Tucson or to stay here when you did."

"Oh, Ken, it's a beautiful ring and very sweet of you for wanting me to have it. I'll accept it, but only on one condition."

"What's that?"

"You have a granddaughter. I know you haven't seen her in long time, but no matter what, when the time comes, I want you to pass it on to her."

"What if I never see her again?"

"You will, Ken, you will. You have to promise me that she will get this ring someday."

"I promise," I said, wondering how I would keep it, and slipped the ring on her finger.

She wore it constantly then, during our days, weeks, months, and years that came and went incredibly fast, filled as they were with love, a lot of laughter, and small adventures. We explored some of Arizona in the RV. She loved all of it, and like everyone, she found the Grand Canyon almost unreal.

I got her into scrapbooking, and in a short time, she was into it with a vengeance. Faster and better than I ever was.

We hiked a couple of times a week and walked every morning we weren't hiking. Two or three times a month, we took my favorite hike. The first time we did, when we got to the highest point, I told her it was mostly downhill from there.

"This is the summit then?"

"For this hike it is. Not for these mountains though."

"I know not for the mountains. For us though, it is now and always will be the summit. It's beautiful. When I die, I want you to spread my ashes here, so when you hike here, we'll be close again. This will be a good place to rest too, when my time comes."

"Okay, if you want me to." I turned my back to her then, not wanting her to see the tears welling in my eyes.

She understood and moved up behind me, put her arms around me, and leaned her head against my back.

"It's okay, Ken," she said. "It'll all be okay."

As soon as I pulled myself together, we started down. It took a while for her words to stop haunting me. We both knew that our time was limited. Her cancer seemed to be under control, it just wasn't gone. We had no idea when the day would come, we only knew it would. And no matter how much time we had, it would never be enough.

The months turned into years, so we got more time than we expected at the start.

Jen and Pete came for visit once. It was mid-March, after the winter rains were heavy. They loved the hikes and had trouble believing the beauty of the desert and mountains, covered as they were with wild flowers.

When we reached the summit on our favorite hike, Peri took my hand, squeezing it to reassure me that everything was still okay.

"This is our special place," she told them. "It belongs to Ken and me. It doesn't matter who else ever comes here, it's still ours."

They stayed a week and we all enjoyed the visit immensely. It was sad to have them leave, yet for Peri and me, the most important thing was the time we had together.

Walt and Marge visited a couple of times too. Both visits were in April. Marge loved the cactus flowers, which were blooming in April. She didn't like to hike, so it took a while to convince her that the easy trails in the cactus forest would only be a walk. Once we got there, she had so much fun taking pictures of the flowers that she didn't notice the walk was over three miles.

We went up on Mount Lemon where, because of the elevation, some of the wild flowers were still blooming. Both visits were great, even though Peri was noticeably tired after their second visit.

The day we knew time was limited was on our morning walk. Peri had trouble finishing it. The next few months, she gradually went downhill. The day the doctor wrote a prescription for some very strong pain pills, we both knew the end was close.

Peri could have gone into hospice care but chose to stay home. I hired a couple of nurses to help. One was there every day during the week, the other on weekends. Peri was on the pain medication for a couple of weeks, constantly growing weaker. Then one morning, she refused to take any more.

"I want to be awake with you for a while, Ken," she said. "If it gets too bad, I'll take more."

I stayed with her then, leaving the chair I sat in only to use the bathroom. I tried to avoid it, but late in the second day, I dosed off for a few minutes. Peri was watching me when I woke up, a small smile on her face. She tried hard to hide the pain, but she'd been off the drugs for over thirty-six hours, so I knew she was hurting a lot.

"Can I get you anything?" I asked.

"No, just give me your hand."

I did, and she squeezed it lightly. It did the same thing for me that it did the first time, all those many long years ago. Only this time it meant a lot more. A hell of a lot more.

"I want you to know, Ken, that I've always loved you. And right now, I love you more than I ever did. These few short years we've had together has been the best time of my life. Don't ever forget that."

She closed her eyes, and I got out of the chair and kissed her lightly.

"I love you Peri," I said.

She continued to hold my hand, as her breathing grew less labored and softer. I thought for a moment that it was a good sign. She was sleeping for the first time since she refused to take any more drugs.

Then her breathing stopped. Peri was gone. I just stood there, thinking about all the times I tried to find her and about how I finally had. Not this time though. Peri was gone from my life forever, and I would never find her again.

She had kept her promise, though, and never left me until she had no choice.

CHAPTER 14

After Peri died, I did all the things one has to do. Her memorial service in Minnesota was scheduled for an evening, so I flew up there that day and drove the rental car directly to the church. As much as I could, I avoided any conversations. I only wanted to talk to Bill, Jen, and Pete, and that was kept to a minimum. I didn't feel strong enough to carry on a real conversation.

After the service, I went to Bill's. He'd been having health problems of his own for a couple of years and looked tired when I got there. He stayed up for quite a while with me anyway.

We talked a lot about when we were young and some about getting old. We both felt a sense of deep loss and talked about the way life kept slipping by, bit by bit and piece by piece. Especially every time someone close left our lives.

Shortly before we called it a night, Bill brought out a bottle of good bourbon.

"I don't think we need a lot of this," he said, pouring us each a generous amount, "but a couple of stiff shots will help both of us get some sleep."

It did.

I slept on his couch that night and flew back to Tucson the next day.

I waited until December to spread Peri's ashes on the summit. I picked the coldest morning we'd had for a long time to go up. I definitely didn't want company. It was a hard enough to do without having someone watch. The last thing I did before going down was tell her I loved her and that I would be back to see her often.

The next few months were simply lonely. I spent as much time in the mountains as my body could stand. And always, I stopped at the summit to talk to Peri. Every time I left it, I wondered if I wouldn't be better off joining her there permanently.

Finally enough time went by to know I had to try to find some kind of life for myself again.

I started thinking about a trip to Minnesota. At least up there, I could visit old friends and maybe not feel quite so gloomy. The night before I was going to leave, Jen called to tell me Bill was in the hospital. She said they thought it was a mild heart attack.

I waited a couple of days before I called Bill at the hospital. He sounded good, his voice was strong, and he was rather cheerful.

"They said I can go home tomorrow," he told me, "and I'll be damn glad to get out of here. The food is terrible."

We talked a little more and I told him I was coming for a visit and that I would be on my way in a couple of days. The RV was already set to go, so all I needed to do was pack a few clothes and load the rest of the things I always took along on a trip.

In the morning after talking to Bill, I felt better than I had for a while. I went on my morning walk and was fixing my breakfast when the phone rang. It was Jen.

"I have some really bad news," she said. "Dad died last night. They think it was another heart attack."

"Oh no. I thought he was doing okay. I talked to him last night and he sounded good."

"We all thought the same thing, Ken. So did his doctors, but even doctors can be wrong. They sure were this time."

We talked a little more about Bill but cut it off short. Jen had a lot more calls to make. I hung up the phone, not feeling good anymore, just a lot of empty.

At that point, the last thing I wanted was to go back to Minnesota for another memorial service. Yet I knew I didn't have a choice. I owed it to Jen to go.

There wasn't a damn thing I could do for her other than be there. Not being there, however, would be taking something away. So I went.

After the service, I drove the RV up to Jen and Pete's, parked it, and stayed for a few days. Everything considered, it was a good visit. I spent a lot of time with their boys and enjoyed every minute with them. I couldn't help wishing they were my grandchildren. And in a way, they almost were. If nothing else, I think I helped, at least temporarily, to fill a void. For them, as well as Jen and Pete.

One night, Jen and I sat outside drinking beer until it was very late, and I told the story of Peri and me.

All she said when I finished was "I'm glad you finally really found her. I know she was happy you did."

I spent a few days visiting some relatives and thought about calling the kid to tell him I was there. I hadn't talked to him since I was there on my mission to find Peri. I decided the hell with it. Too much time had passed with no contact of any kind. I was sure it was too late to try.

Back in Tucson, the house felt like a hollow shell, devoid of life. I did everything I could to stay busy, hiking a lot, scrapbooking everything, even though my heart wasn't in any of it. I even took on a few carpenter jobs to stay busy. The one thing couldn't stand was to be idle.

I had to be very physically tired to sleep at night. Somehow, I muddled through the next few months.

One day, I hiked to the summit, only because I felt some kind of strong need to be there. I spent a little extra time there, wondering why I made the hike when I was as tired as I was.

As I was getting ready for bed late that night, I suddenly remembered it was a year to the day since Peri died. I fell asleep thinking about her and started to dream immediately.

Mary was there first though. She was out in the field picking tomatoes. She smiled when I joined her, then said, "It was a good thing you did with Peri. She needed you as much as you needed her. Everything is still good between you and me, Ken. It always will be. I just hope you can find something now during this hard time you're having. You still have a lot of years left to live. There is one thing wrong in your life, though, that you have to make right. Do your best with it."

"Mary, I—" I started to say, but she was gone and the phone was ringing in the living room.

"Hi, Ken," Peri said, "I just called to see how you're doing."

"I'm okay," I told her. "But how are you, Peri, how are you really?"

I woke up before she could answer. I sat up on the edge of the bed, soaked in a cold sweat. In those next few moments, I understood what it feels like to be truly alone.

"Where the hell do I go from here?" I wondered.

I tried to go back to sleep. It was totally impossible. I got dressed and went out to the back patio with a cup of coffee. I don't know how long I was there, watching the stars and listening to a couple of coyotes howling out in the park, before the moon started rising. It was nearly full and lit up the night. I knew then what I had to do. I'd always wanted to make a moonlight hike, I just never had the courage before. Now was the time. I quickly got my gear together and was on my way.

Any other time and I knew I'd be very nervous walking the trails alone, with everything around covered in dark shadows. Often, I could hear the night critters around, even though I couldn't see any of them.

A few times, where the shadows were the heaviest, I nearly lost the trail. It somehow didn't bother me. I felt almost as if something was guiding me. I knew I would make it safely to the summit.

I reached it at first light. It was good then to stop for a rest. I turned back and looked at the desert down below. It carried a soft, warm glow in the dim light.

A few thin, fluffy clouds started moving in, and as the sun hit them, the sky filled with brilliant reds and golds. I took a lot of pictures in a different light than I'd ever had up there.

As I watched the sun come up, it reminded me once again that sunrise is always a good time to be alive. Especially when you're out and about. And this time, I knew Peri was watching it with me, very close by.

Sunrise always means another new day, another chance, and for me, maybe, just maybe, another new start at living. No matter what, there is always a good reason to do that. After all, that's what Mary said she wanted for me, and I knew Peri did too.

When I got off the mountain and home, I was extremely tired. It was a long hike after going with almost no sleep. Yet I felt refreshed and stronger than I'd felt for a long time. I knew then that nothing was going to be easy, but no matter what, I'd make it through. There was something, some reason, for me to live out whatever natural life I had left.

I wasn't in the house long before the phone rang. I was unloading the hiking gear and cameras from the car and had to run to catch it before it stopped ringing.

"Hey, Dad," the kid said when I answered. "It's been a long time since we've talked to each other. I know it's my fault. It's taken me a long time to finally get the guts to call you to tell you I'm sorry. The kids and Gladys have been after me to call too. They've missed you a lot. We all want to come down there to see you soon, if it's okay?"

It was.

CPSIA information can be obtained
at www.ICGtesting.com
Printed in the USA
LVHW091621060520
655116LV00003B/965